FEAR

of the

MIND

Martha Perez

FEAR OF THE MIND
Copyright © 2018 Martha Perez

ISBN- 13: 978-0-9998843-7-9
ISBN- 10: 0-9998843-7-9

Cover Design by The Book Khaleesi

In Loving Memory of Our Beloved Son

Rudy S. Andalon

3/22/1979 - 3/14/2017

Contents

The Power of the Mind 1

Fantasy Man Tell Lies 3

The House on the Hill 5

Mind Games 38

What Were You Thinking 71

Dark Mountain 100

A Brother's Betrayal 134

Unsane 152

Trust 171

Winning Ticket 188

Gentlemen's Club 211

Other Titles by Martha Perez 249

About the Author 251

The Power of the Mind

T here's a mystery man, staring at me in my mind; like a distorted mirror reflection peering back at me, fears begin to take shape in my mind as I try to fight them. Tears roll down my cheeks as I sit uncomfortably on the floor of a lonely, unknown room underground. It's a dark and strange place where the only audible sound is that of water cascading down the walls to a hole in the ground beneath; a hole beneath, spiraling staircase above, it's a poignant juxtaposition. I sit on the damp floor with fear enveloping me like a blanket on a cold *winter morning. It paralyzes me to the point that I cannot move even if I tried. I keep the trap door shut most of the time for fear of falling into the deep hole from which there's no coming back alive. My inner self is trapped in this basement, the only place where my fears are free to roam but never un-chained; it makes me scared and alive at the same time. My little secret will die with me and that's no lie.*

Fantasy Man Tell Lies

*Y*ou *are an attention-grabbing mystery man, an enigma; a figment of my imagination that's best ignored. If I fuel this dark fantasy by giving it more thought and energy than it deserves, you'll feel validated; and then there'll be no end to the mind games you play with me. You slither smoothly in the fertile ground of my memories and imagination like a venomous rattlesnake in a bid to steal my heart, capture my soul and poison my body. I know you'd not leave my dreams alone but I won't let you take them from me. I may be naïve but*

MARTHA PEREZ

I'm also fearless. There's a hidden fire that burns within me and it can destroy you; I'll leave you in ashes and you wouldn't even know how you were consumed. I won't turn back when I leave everything behind and take back the peace you stole from me. I'm no longer the helpless queen in your checkered mind game of lies.

The House on the Hill

There's a house on the top of a hill in a quaint little county where an old couple once lived. They were killed in a gruesome murder when they were in their late eighties; the killer was never found even though stories about the house and the couple went around town like a never dying fire. The house was now abandoned with no buyers, and was in an unkept state. The air hung heavily in deathly silence around the house and people were afraid of going there. But both children and adults alike were curious about the house and its premises. Despite several warnings not to approach or lurk near the house, no one listens. Just last week two teens were found dead, stiff as a board in the backyard of the house. I keep telling folks that the house is off-limits before any more people get killed. My name is Jessica Morgan and I'm a detective in charge of resolving the mystery surrounding this old couple's ghastly murder. When it happened nearly a decade ago, it had shaken the community as such incidents were unheard of in an otherwise quiet town where people lived in peace.

Resolving this case and bringing closure to it is important for me as an investigator but there's something else which I've been unable to make sense of. I've had dreams of this house for years before I even got appointed to the case or knew anything about it. In the dream, I'm dressed in a plain white cotton dress and someone's chasing me in this very house whereas in real life, until my official appointment, I've never been in this house or its premises or even this town for that matter. When I first came to this house to have a look around before I began my investigation, I felt goose bumps because of the realization that this was the house that kept appearing in my dreams. I still haven't a clue about what the connection is but I'm determined to bring an end to this case.

I'm at my office desk with papers and files accumulated over the years regarding this case. I'll need a jug of coffee to just get through all this paperwork and glean information from it. Some of these files contain rather disturbing, grotesque details about the murder scene;

things which are considered gold for an investigator; but for me, it makes me squirm in my seat and seethe with anger at the audacity & repulsive mind of the killer. There's a whole file on how investigators had found teenage girls chained to the roof of the basement of this house, or whatever was left of their bodies because they were badly mutilated with an axe; their body parts were found in a leather suitcase. As I scour the pages in the file on the girls, I see an uncanny resemblance to the old couple's decade old murder in the basement of the same house. The girls were not related to the couple in any way but this house had become a hotspot. It was like a sacred ritual ground for whoever was behind the murders because all the killings had the same forensic markings pointing to a single killer, possibly male who's well versed in han-

dling an axe.

In the old couple's murder, it's believed that Harold Park was awakened by some noise coming from below because despite having severe arthritis, he walked down the stairs to the basement late in the night only to be stabbed multiple times by the killer until the blade of the axe broke off. Jane Park was fast asleep in the bedroom upstairs and was unaware of the killer's presence in the house. Bloody footprints were found going up from the basement to the upstairs bedroom where Jane Park was. Her body was found on the bed with an axe firmly lodged in her head, making a fatal cut down the center of her forehead and eyes. Her body didn't show any signs of struggle or any marks elsewhere to indicate any attempts from her to escape. The investigators concluded that the couple may have known the killer closely and may possibly be even related, though as of now, it's unconfirmed. Why anyone would murder an old, harmless couple is unfathomable but the grotesque manner in which it's been done begs the question. What was the motive? It was certainly not a random kill. Was it for thrill? Could it be revenge? Did the killer hold a personal vendetta against the old couple or was he a psycho serial killer that was seeking to quench his thirst for power or control?

I look at the family tree as I search for more details, these questions need to be answered and they made me restless. They had a son who died two years ago before they were murdered. The old couple had a grandson,

FEAR OF THE MIND

named Tom Park; he had no residential address listed in the detail section but there was a small scribble in red beside his name that said 'homeless'. He's often found wandering around the bridge under the freeway downtown and is presumed to live there. He sometimes visited his grandparents when they were alive. He's known to have been a bright student and had good grades at school so how he ended up becoming a vagabond was a subject of interest. I grab some coffee before I sit down to read more on Tom Park. I have a feeling that meeting this man might be necessary to gauge him and perhaps speaking to him may yield new clues. I give the cops on my team a heads-up about bringing him to the office tomorrow for a tête-à-tête.

MARTHA PEREZ

It's a bright and cool Thursday morning as I make my way to the bureau head office. Today I'll get a chance to sit face to face with Tom Park and I was looking forward to it. Past investigators viewed him as a likely suspect but had no luck in finding any evidence against him. I prep my mind going over questions that I'd like to ask him through my 20-minute drive.

I get to the office bustling with activity as is routine on a week day; everything from suicide, homicide, theft, conspiracy and the whole assortment of crimes come to a head under this roof. I head straight for the coffee machine, eager to get some hot brew down my throat and get this day started when my eyes catch a poorly dressed, lanky man seated at the chair next to my desk. He looks up and catches me seeing him. I turn back to the machine and pick up two cups of coffee and head toward my desk.

"Tom Park?" I ask holding out a cup of coffee to him.

"Yes, that would be me" he said, inhaling the aroma of the warm brew. He promptly takes the cup from me, eager to gulp the hot liquid.

I take my seat and watch him take sips.

He looks up and gives a faint smile.

"I don't get to drink a hot cup of coffee every day, so this is a real treat" he said, continuing to sip his coffee.

I wave my hand to say 'no worries' and decide to get straight to the purpose of the meeting.

"Mr. Park, I have some questions for you

which I hope you'd answer to the best of your ability and recollection. I'm sure you're sufficiently apprised by the officers as to why you're here at my desk today"

"Yes, I do." He replied his fingers tightly laced around his cup.

I continue.

"Your grandparents Mr. & Mrs. Park were killed at 1818, North Gateway ten years ago. It's the only house located on the hill and visitors were few. You and your father being the most frequent in that visitor list."

I pause to gauge his reaction and see his face begin to redden with anger and frustration.

"What do you want to know? I didn't kill them!" he says throwing his hands in the air in exasperation.

FEAR OF THE MIND

"I never said you did Mr. Park. Our past investigations regarding your grandparents' murder has determined that the killer was someone who they knew closely. Do you suspect anyone?"

"No" he said, calmly.

"Where were you when they were killed?" I ask in the hope he'd say something different from the alibi he'd given in past interviews.

He gave me a cold stare but continued to be calm. Whether the calm he was exhibiting was that of a criminal who knew he'd never been caught or of someone who was telling the truth & had nothing more to lose, was another matter altogether.

"I was staying in my corner under the bridge where I live" he said.

Damn, I muttered under my breath. He's

been through numerous interviews like this one. If he's a seasoned criminal, by now he must have polished his answers and countenance to fool investigators into thinking he had nothing do with the subject of the investigation. His demeanor was giving nothing away and frustration was beginning to creep in my voice.

I tap my fingers on the desk impatiently, wondering if there were any areas of questioning that my peers would've left out during their interviews with him. There were bloodied footprints from the stairs in the crime scene that are filed in the database. The shoe size of the killer is shown to be a size ten.

"What's your shoe size Mr. Park?" I ask looking straight into his eyes.

"I wouldn't know. I'm a homeless man

with barely a shirt on my back. I don't have the luxury of having shoes, toiletries or anything of my own." He says nonchalantly.

So far, he hasn't wavered even once but now I'm sensing a slight nervousness as his eyes are gazing downward, unable to meet my eyes.

I take my card and hand it over to him. "Let me know if you remember anything or want to tell me something that may help resolve this

case and find your grandparent's killer"

He takes it and looks at it. Then looks up and says "Yeah."

"You can call me anytime," I say as he gets up to leave.

"Sure," he says and then walks out, relieved to be out of my scrutiny.

MARTHA PEREZ

I get up to get another cup of coffee and see him exiting the office building. He maintained a fairly calm manner throughout except for that one trace of nervousness I detected when I asked his shoe size. My instincts picked up on his nervousness quickly but I didn't want to press him. It was my first meeting with him and something told me that it wouldn't be the last time I'd be seeing him.

I finish the day eager to get home. I get into the car and start driving when I suddenly feel the urge to drive to the house on the hill; may be seeing the crime scene again will bring some information to light. I get home and change into a pair of old jeans and a navy-blue tee. I take a quick bite of my favorite pulled pork sandwich and head out the door back to my car. It's a little past nine pm when I drive uphill; it's about ten minutes to get to the house from there. I get close to the house and see a faint light emitting from one of the rooms of the house as if someone had lit a candle.

'Who could it be at this hour?' I whispered to myself as I grab my gun, flashlight & pepper spray and step out of the car. I begin walking towards the house slowly, careful not to make any sound. I suddenly feel a pair of hands catch me from behind and I turn around and punch the person down. I see a man fall to the ground covering his face. I get ready to hit him once more when he uncovers his face.

To my surprise, it's Tom.

"What are you doing here?" he says, still wincing in pain from the hit.

"I could ask you the same thing" I say and pull him up.

"I come here every few months" he said. I can see the right side of his face become a sickly purple from the bruise I've inflicted on him.

"So you lit a candle?" I say pointing in the direction of the faint light I'd seen when I was getting here.

"No, I never do. I saw the candlelight too but didn't have the courage to step in. Someone's in there but I don't know who it could be. I thought I and Dad were the only ones who visited grandpa and grandma when they were alive".

"This may be our only chance at finding out who's in there and I have a strong feeling it's the killer of your grandparents who's in there" I say pointing my gun forward.

"I'm scared, this is nuts." Tom says as his

face now has an expression of both fear and pain.

"I'm here, you don't have to be scared, come on now," I say as I cautiously walk forward to the front door which is partially open. Tom follows behind me. I'm convinced that I was barking at the wrong tree because Tom is clearly not the killer unless he does a 180 on me. I look over my shoulders and nod him to step inside the house first.

We take ten steps inside when I feel someone hit me from behind with a heavy object. I drop my flashlight as I blank out and drop to the floor. When I open my eyes, I look up and around; I'm lying in the basement and next to me, there's Tom who also seems to have been knocked out unconscious. I turn on my side and decide to take a pulse; I feel nothing but he lay motionless and unconscious as if he was dead. The dingy basement which was beginning to resemble a nightmare I've been having for years. I remember the dream, in flashes; was this going to be the end of the road for me? Will I die tonight? Like this? I shake my head, fighting the thoughts that were threatening my sanity and willpower. Every move I make from here on is a life or death situation.

My head is wincing with pain from the hit I'd taken. I was struggling to see clearly in the darkness of the basement but then suddenly, I hear the sound of someone walking down the staircase. I knew that was the killer and I was trying hard to see who it was. My eyes widened in horror as I see it's a woman! Did the Park family have a daughter or a sister the public didn't know about? There was nothing

FEAR OF THE MIND

on the case file about a woman, not even a female friend.

I try to take a closer look at the woman
who's now standing and gazing down at me
like I was prey. She was Caucasian, in her mid
50's, of medium built and about 5ft 6' tall. She
had wavy ash blonde hair and even in this
poorly lit basement, her green eyes twinkled
with pure evil.

"You didn't have to kill Tom" I say, wondering what my next move should be. Engag-
ing in conversation with a potential killer buys
time
enough to escape or avert danger.

"Give me one good reason why? He's a
homeless punk and I was doing him a favor by
putting him out of his misery" she snorted as

she began walking around me like a vulture circling its meal.

"Who are you and why are you here?" I ask.

I continue... "They don't have a daughter and both Mr. & Mrs. Park don't have a sister listed in the contact info provided for their family and closest relatives"

"You know, you got this picture all wrong," she said as she pulled a chair to sit beside me. I try sitting up on the floor; my head is swollen and my body feels weak. I knew if I had a chance to make it out of here alive, it's to use the training I've been given. However, I admit, even I didn't see this coming. A woman was not even

in the frame of this investigation.

"You see Miss Morgan, Mr. Park had a

lover back then. She was hot and horny while he was old and had the energy of a bull. Sadly, for him, Mrs. Park was simply not interested in getting caught up in lusty after dark leisure activities. Mr. Park suffered from severe arthritis but when you're old and horny, nothing hurts! He took fancy to this hot middle-aged cougar and had sex with her all the time. She quite enjoyed it and became addicted to his passionate energy. There's a reason why old wine tastes so good. That lover was me. I wanted to marry him and become Mrs. Park but then he wouldn't leave the old hag he called his wife. He didn't like disturbing the status quo and this enraged me. One night, I decided to change the status quo and put an end to it. It didn't require any meticulous planning, he was old and had arthritis, there couldn't have been a more vulnerable victim. I went to his house that night and stayed in the basement; this is where we often spend hours having hot sex and Mrs. Park thought he was fixing the pipe! He came down the stairs thinking I was going to undress for him; instead I hugged him and stabbed him first with a knife. There lay an axe in the basement which I decided needed to be put to good use. So I hit him with the axe the next time till his body lay in pieces. It felt better than an orgasm. I then went upstairs to finish the most important part of this masterpiece, killing Mrs. Park. If she was out of the picture, everything would've been fine. Now that you've heard this entertaining story Ms. Morgan, I have to kill you too. I'm too old to be spending my remaining days in a prison and die there."

FEAR OF THE MIND

Saying this, she gets up from her seat and walks toward me.

My body suddenly stiffens, wondering what she's going to do. I had to figure something out.

She gets closer, a butcher knife in hand and then speaks as if in a whisper "You shouldn't get too nosy Ms. Morgan"

This was my chance. I raise my hand quickly and punch her in the face. She stumbles and falls backward taking the full impact of my fist.

From the corner of my eye I see a figure quickly moving in the shadow screaming "Mother!"

I grab the knife from the lunatic woman who is now on the floor and quickly get into attack mode. It isn't going to be easy trying to fight a potential killer in such poor light. And this was no time to search for my flashlight.

The mysterious figure is still blotted out in darkness so I take a step forward, my fingers grasping the handle of the knife ever so tightly. A bead of sweat rolls down my forehead.

"I'll kill her in no time, you better step forward and show yourself, I'm sure you'll agree that this isn't the time for your crazy games because it isn't going to work" I say loudly into the darkness.

Suddenly I feel a pair of hands come from my left to grab my neck, I deliver a deep cut on the killer's forearm, deep enough to have blood gushing out like a burst pipe. And then kick his stomach.

I see the mysterious figure collapse on the

woman and see a dim light streaming from above the staircase on his face. I gasped in horror, it was Tom!

If this wasn't a life or death situation, the sight before me would've seemed almost comical. Two fully grown adults were one on top of another. My instincts hadn't failed me about Tom but I wish I recognized it sooner. The crazy woman who was having an affair with Mr. Park was none other than Tom's mother; Mr. Park was having an affair with his own daughter in law?! This was scandalous and shocking. I grab my cell phone and ring the head office for backup, my mind still warped by the ugly narrative underlying these murders. It doesn't end there. Mother and son were mentally ill and showed signs of receiving abnormal psychological gratification by the heinous crimes they committed, including raping and murdering the girls found chain to the basement; who knows how more skeletons will rattle out of their murder closet.

As I lose myself momentarily thinking of the charges to file against them on multiple counts, I feel someone grab my ankle. I turn around to see Tom's hand firmly gripping my leg, just my luck! I kick and try to free myself. I lose balance and fall down. Tom lets go off my ankle and positions himself over me and presses my neck.

"I killed my grandparents for their life insurance. It wasn't my Mum; she was trying to protect me. Of course, she had fun with my grandpa but I had the pleasure of ending his life. I thought I'll get the insurance money for myself but turns out the dirty old man had do-

FEAR OF THE MIND

nated his insurance savings to an orphanage."

"So that's all there was to this, some cash?" I struggle to say as I continue to pry his hands from my neck.

"Yeah, things don't have to always be so complicated darling; you're a feisty piece of work. I think I'm going to enjoy killing you" he says with an evil grin.

"You better hurry up then because the cops are already on their way, you wouldn't want to get tied up in handcuffs now, do you?" I say as I bite try to bite off his finger.

"Arghhh ouch!!! You bitch, I'm going to finish you" he snarled as he picked up an old baseball bat lying around in the basement.

I was bracing myself for a hit and curl my body into a fetal position to protect my vital organs from getting damaged. I want to come out of this alive. I'm going to survive this. I see Tom swinging the bat in the air as if he was going to hit a ball out of the park, but it was coming down to hit me.

I see the butcher knife lying next to me and grab it before he swings the bat down and start stabbing Tom's legs. He stumbles to the ground, dropping the bat to the floor. He recovers quickly and then punches me in my face. I had forgotten that I had a gun strapped in my ankle holster as backup. I reach down for it and shoot it at Tom, whose face was a mix of shock and fear. I keep firing shots till I hear a flurry of footsteps come down the stairs; the cops were finally here and one of them grabs my gun from me. I collapse into a chair drained by the ordeal. They get the paramedics and clear the basement. Tom had taken four bullets, one in his shoulder, two in his legs and one in his right side. His mother was unconscious but alive at the time of being taken to the hospital while Tom was taken straight to the OR. I escape with minor injuries to my face, stomach and head and get treated by the paramedics on scene.

I explain to my seniors what transpired and gave as much detail as I could remember. The case was finally closed two months later; both Tom and his crazy mother pleaded guilty and confessed to the murders of Mr. & Mrs. Park and the three girls raped & killed, chained to the basement. They were given life sentences on multiple counts of murder including an attempt to murder an investigating officer. I was present at the court room hearing and was relieved to see the two lunatics behind bars for life, that's one less headache to deal with.

Even though Tom and his mother confessed to the murder of his grandparents and the girls, they pleaded not guilty for the murder of the young teenage boy. Because the crime took place in the backyard of the same house of horrors, it would've been reasonable to presume that they were also responsible for that. But there was no motive in the murder of the boy, no evidence and no confession of crime. I had to go back to the drawing board on resolving the mystery of this young lad's murder but it was disturbing beyond words could tell. Did this mean that there was another killer on the loose?

I decide to drive back to the house on the

hill. Here we go again. In the course of two months of wrapping up the investigation, I made multiple trips to and from the crime scene with forensic experts and other officers from the bureau. By now, I'm familiar with the route uphill and go only during the day. If a killer was on the loose, I didn't want a repeat of that night again. I knew I had to be careful because now my name was out in the public when news of these crimes made it to the paper.

In the midst of dark details and gory murders, I forgot how scenic this route uphill had been during the day. It was lonely, but it was also peaceful and untouched; the road was narrow and the climb was steep even for a hill but the views on the way up and down were breathtaking.

MARTHA PEREZ

I finally get there and park my car on the side. The last time I was here, it was 3 weeks ago, just two days before the murder convictions for Tom and his mother were given. The house looks the same and the yellow crime scene tapes were still on. However, I see something red painted on the outside wall of the house, something that wasn't there on my last visit. I tip toe around and get closer to see what it is. A chill runs down my spine when I see the wall. 'You are dead Jessica Morgan' was etched in what seems like red paint.

The killer knew I'd come here which means he's familiar with my movements or he's tracking me in some way. He wanted me to see this, to let me know that he was watching me or that I was next on his list. I speed dial my assistant at the head office and give a

FEAR OF THE MIND

heads up to get a forensic team here ASAP. The paint was still partially wet which means the killer was here just a short time ago; the forensic team would feast on this as the possibility of fresh fingerprints and evidence is positively thrilling.

My   work   is   never   done.

Mind Games

My alarm rings at 6am and I'm annoyed by its loyalty to wake people up. It's Saturday morning and my weekend off. I could do with the break and unwind but I fear a migraine is coming for me as I have a splitting headache to contend with. I lie in bed a few minutes more and look toward my window. The sky is a beautiful pale golden pink, the sun just beginning to rise over the horizon. I take in the picturesque sight in my half-asleep state and for a moment, the headache doesn't seem so bad. I finally push myself to the edge of the bed, stretch and stand up. I think I need to pop an aspirin before this headache gets any worse. I walk to the kitchen and plop myself over the stool and pour myself a glass of water. I need to head to the market to buy a few groceries and stock up my fridge for the busy week ahead.

I take a quick shower and change into a plain midi-length dress, a welcome change from the usual jeans, trousers and tees I wear through the week. I take a look at myself in the mirror. At 35, I'm in fairly good shape; I'm 5ft 7', a natural brunette and petite framed. I grab my handbag and put on a pair of black sunglasses before I walk out the door.

As I walk down the street, I bump straight into someone's chest. I look up and see a tall

dark and handsome man looking down at me;
I
flush embarrassed and step back.

"I'm sorry" I say.

"It's okay pretty lady" he says with a grin.

I look at him again. He's dressed in dark denims and a tee which says 'Hawaii' on it, covered in tropical print. He has short dark hair and a warm tanned complexion. However, what struck me were his eyes, they were a mix of hazel and brick brown, like molten gold and copper mixed together. I shake myself of my observation when I notice him looking at me in the same way.

"You've got gorgeous eyes" he says with a gentle smile.

I blush and suddenly it just becomes all awkward. What on earth was I doing talking to a complete stranger?! I was behaving like an idiot. His countenance was welcoming and put me at ease; but there was something else that I couldn't put my finger on. And it was making me anxious enough to feel my muscles tense up. It was just this odd familiar feeling like we've known each other when clearly this was the first time I was seeing him. I see him picking up fruits that had fallen from my bag but something makes me want to get away from there, so I turn back quickly and break into a jog as if I was going to catch a train.

"Hey where you going?" I hear him call out with a laugh that makes it all the more uncomfortable. I run all the way home and quickly lock all doors. I'm still breathless as I'm drawing the curtains at my window when to my horror, I see him outside staring at my house. He followed me home?! WTF. Was he a stalker? I head down to my basement with my cell phone, hoping he'd be gone. I could call 911 but this is just the first time; I had to give this guy the benefit of doubt because his motive for following me all the way home was still unclear.   My whole body is drained and I collapse onto an old couch in the basement and fell asleep.

I wake up after what seems like a few hours; groggy eyed, I head upstairs to see dawn breaking over a new day. I slept in the basement through the whole of yesterday?! Ugh. I open the curtains and see folks in my neighborhood head out for their morning run. Autumn was making its presence known as it's chilly outside, and dried yellow leaves were being swept away with the early morning breeze. The guy from the market was nowhere in sight. I sigh in relief and head to the kitchen to make myself a cup of coffee.

A few hours later, I'm feeling hungry and decide to eat lunch at a local restaurant not too far away. I've heard they serve the best chicken fried steak and it's a must try. I change into a pair of straight fit denims and a forest green tee. It's half past 12 when I finally step out the house and drive to the restaurant. It's not too crowded for Sunday lunch when I step in, I head straight for the discreet corner table. The waitress heads over to my table ready to take my order with a dirty apron on, messy hair, wearing reading glasses, and chewing a huge piece of gum. OMG what a sight to behold. Anyway, I order chicken fried steak and some mashed potatoes, no gravy and some coffee.

MARTHA PEREZ

I'm waiting for my order and look outside the window that I see him. It's the guy from the market, and he has a raven sitting on his arm. My muscles begin to tense again and a strong feeling of nausea takes over. I call the waitress and tell her to pack my order and head to the restroom. In the rest room, I wash my face and take a couple of deep breaths to release any pent-up tension in my body. The best way to step out the restaurant is to go through the back door or the fire exit. I step out of the restroom and see the waitress coming out the kitchen with my order. I wave her in my direction, her eyes widen with concern. I hand her the cash for my order and ask her to point me to the fire exit. My car was parked on the other side of the road which now feels like a blessing in disguise. I head out the exit and hurry to my car, keys and my food order in hand. I drive back home feeling sick to my stomach and clueless as to why this man was following me around. I'm overwhelmed with fear and my body is trembling. I knew these were the signs of a panic attack so I try to stay as calm as possible and drive slowly. I wanted to get home in one piece. I reach home and head straight to my kitchen to drink some water. I felt like a scared little child; I go to my bedroom and change into casual clothes. I didn't eat my lunch because I lost my appetite. I close the curtains and retreat to my bed for a noontime nap, in the hope that I'll feel better when I wake up.

Suddenly, I wake up breathless and panicking. I get out of bed and walk through all the rooms to make sure no one's there. It was a bad dream, I felt like someone was trying to strangle me. My mind is acting up because of my anxiety and fears. I feel like I'm going crazy. Fuck! I hate feeling so vulnerable. I walk to the living room to open the curtains. I see it's dark outside and look quickly at the wall clock, it reads half past 6. I look out the window again and everything seems normal but then again, it doesn't. I see dozens of ravens sitting over the trees lining the footpath outside my house. This was most unusual as I haven't seen anything like this around here before. I wasn't the superstitious kind but I've heard stories like seeing ravens were bad luck or were a sign of death in the family, either yours or someone you love.

Maybe I'm going crazy. I close the curtains again trying to push out all irrational thoughts and fears from my mind. I hear a knock on my front door. I feel my muscles tense up again, fearful of whom I'd find at my doorstep. I wasn't expecting any visitors. I open the door and my eyes widen in horror, it's the same guy from the market. I feel a sudden surge of courage and step forward and look straight into his eyes.

"What the hell do you want? Why are you following me around like this? Do you really fancy being put behind bars for harassing me?" I ask in an angry, frustrated voice.

"Well you called me, darling" he said with a faint smile dancing on his lips.

"What? Why on earth would I call you? I haven't even seen you before in my life and don't know you. I haven't called you so stop making up stories now!" I say, repulsed by the audacity of his answer.

"You call me every year around Halloween, darling; don't you think your mind is playing tricks on you to disbelieve what I'm saying? But the truth is that your fears and nightmares are all about to come true." He says with an evil grin.

"Halloween? What's that got to do with anything?! I don't know what you're talking about! Stop wasting my time and get out of here" I yell.

"You know exactly what I'm talking about. And if you have any plans on pretending otherwise, soon you'll know that everything comes to an end sweetie"

"I'm not your sweetie" and slam the door shut to his face. I rush to pick up my cell phone to the call the cops, but something told me not to do it. I turn around to check whether he's still lurking around on my front porch and see no one. Was this guy really here or was he just a figment of my imagination?! I didn't hear any vehicle park near my house, and neither did I hear one leave. How did he get here? What was he saying about Halloween? That I called him? He's lost his mind.

Halloween is tomorrow and there's a lot of mischief this time of the year. Something odd struck me about him. Throughout the conversation, he maintained a sage like calm and my aggressive countenance was in stark contrast to his.

I spend a few minutes walking back and forth in my living room and when I'm convinced he isn't around, I head to the kitchen counter to unpack my lunch order which is going to be tonight's dinner. I go over our exchange in my mind while I reheat it. I pour myself a glass of red wine; I could do with a couple of glasses to relax.

The chicken fried steak lived up to its hype;
the mashed potato was buttery, light and creamy though I now regret not having ordered some gravy. After wiping my plate clean and finishing two glasses of wine, I settle on a bar of dark chocolate flavored with roast almonds and dry fruits for dessert. Good food and great wine is an instant mood booster but the mystery surrounding this man was deepening. I didn't know where to start and how it was going to end. Though my stomach was

FEAR OF THE MIND

full, I was feeling emotionally spent and drained. I needed to get a good night's sleep.

I change into night clothes after my shower and slip under my bedcovers, hoping to finally close my eyes and just sleep minus the nightmares and panic attacks.

I don't know whether this is a dream but it feels real; I hear a man's voice whisper to me, 'Baby it's time to be together, how I wait for this time every year to be with you.' I can feel someone's mouth lick and kiss my ears. I toss and turn in my bed, partially turned on & partially fearful. I feel someone's tongue down my neck and suddenly open my eyes wide to see who it is. There's no one?!! I was dreaming, again! It's 6.30am on my bedside clock and today's Halloween.

The call goes through, "Hello?"

"Eddie, it's me, Martina. I'm thinking of remote working today, feeling a bit off. Would you hold things together there for me?"

"Don't worry, Martina, I've got you covered" he quips.

"Thanks, Eddie, you are a true friend and business partner." I say, relieved.

"You take care Martina, see ya tomorrow, between, Happy Halloween!" he says.

"Happy Halloween Eddie, get going, there's enough to do"

"Bye, Martina."

"Bye, Eddie."

While cooking dinner, I hear a knock my door. I open to see a bunch of children dressed in their Halloween best with little bags to collect candies. I happily fill their bags with the candies and wish them 'Happy Halloween'.

FEAR OF THE MIND

What a joyful bunch, it's a sight for sore eyes. I close the door behind me and head back to the kitchen when I hear another knock. I open the door and to my utter surprise, it's the mystery guy!

'Happy Halloween' he says smiling from ear to ear and walks right in as if this was his house.

"Your house smells delicious, just like you, what's cooking darlin?" he says as he heads to the dining area.

I follow him there, visibly relaxed and ask him,

"What are you doing here?"

"Well you invited me for dinner, don't you remember?" he quips.

"Excuse me? But I haven't invited you for dinner." I say, completely taken aback by his answer.

He heads to the shelf adjacent to the dining table and takes out my cherished three tier candlebra & lights the candles in it with a lighter he took from his jeans pocket. I can't believe it. He was setting up the table for dinner like he knew this house and where things were kept. He looks up at me smiling. It's like I've known him for a lifetime, and this right here felt like deja-vu. I give him a smile back, his calmness soothing my nerves. I turn to the kitchen to plate out dinner for both of us as if this was the natural thing to do.

"Why do you call me 'mysterious guy', I'm not a mystery to you Martina." He says as he hovers around me in the kitchen.

FEAR OF THE MIND

How did he know I didn't call him a mystery guy out loud? I thought it to myself.

"I have not an inkling as to why I'm entertaining a perfect stranger in my house!" I say, exasperated as I begin to assemble the roast chicken onto a serving plate, playing along his game.

He grabs me by my shoulder and looks deeply into my eyes as if he was speaking words through them. I look at him, speechless by the beauty of his eyes and the strength I feel from his body. He then takes my hand and caresses my fingers with his lips. He then begins to suck them slowly like he was licking off the juices of the roast chicken off my fingers. It's pleasurable to the point where my face is flushed, the sensation of his mouth on my fingers is nothing short of wild. Truth is, I didn't want him to stop and I don't resist when he closes in near my neck and sticks his tongue into my ear and licks me down my neck. I've felt this sensation before, in my dream! He stops and then looks up at me, I'm wide eyed and motionless in the kitchen dwarfed by this gentle giant standing before me, all 6ft 2 of him. My body responds with craving, not for roast chicken but for him as he gauges my reaction to his teasing touch. He grabs me by the waist and then does the same thing to my other ear, circling his tongue inside it and then leaving a trail of kisses down the nape of my neck. I'm turned on and run my fingers through his hair and then he looks at me again, pleased with my response.

"You know me from before Martina, don't deny it. You've been here with me before, you

FEAR OF THE MIND

know me from your dreams darlin, I'm no stranger. Don't you feel that we've known each other? I know the curves in your body and what delights your senses, I know your body is craving me right now, but you'll have to wait for it" he says as he tucks a strand of hair from my loose bun behind my ears.

I take my eyes off him and turn back to plate the dinner. I'm trying to stay calm but I can feel a thrill, a rush of something deliciously seductive rising in my body. He was right, I was craving him and I knew him from my dream, but who was he really? What kind of sorcery was this? I feel his fingers wrap around my waist as he delicately touches my belly and goes upward to cup my breasts. And then he plants another kiss near my neck. I'm melting under his gaze and touch like candle wax.

"Let's eat some dinner before it gets cold" he says as he steps back and carries the tray of roast chicken to the table. He was playing games with me and I was loving every bit of it thus far. All fears and caution went flying out the window. I was at ease and wet inside, begging and pleading for more. We sit facing each other, helping ourselves to the delicious spread. He holds his glass of Moscato to toast and I raise mine in response, wondering what else this evening holds.

He looks at me intently as he takes one bite after another of the roast chicken, with a mischievous smile dancing around his lips. I see his collar bones protruding from under his shirt and look at his Adam's apple and gulp down another sip of wine. He was a visual treat for the eyes and I was feasting not just on the chicken, but also him. He helps me clean up after dinner and moistens my cheek with a soft kiss when we're in the kitchen.

"I'll be waiting for dessert" he said giving me a wink and heads back to the living room.

I'm playing along not knowing how all this is going to end. I slice up some warm carrot cake with cream cheese icing for dessert and carry the dessert plates to the living room. He's tending to the fire he's got going in the fire-place. His eyes sparkle with passion as I nervously place the tray in front of him. He motions me to sit down next to him and scoops up a spoon of the creamy icing and holds it to my mouth. I swallow it hungrily and feel like he's giving me a foretaste of what's to come. We spend the next few minutes eating dessert in quiet silence in the backdrop of a crackling fireplace. He gets up when I'm still scraping the last bits of my cake from the plate and goes to the cd player close by. He puts on some jazz music and walks in my direction; he sits down next to me and removes the hair stick that held my hair together in a bun. Now my hair has dropped into a bunch of loose curls over my shoulder and he brushes a few strands away from my face.

"I've missed you" he says as he caresses my face with his fingers.

"Will you dance with me?" he pleads as he holds out his hands to me.

I nod in silence and keep my hand in his. He holds me by my waist as I feel his strength in every part of my body. I want him inside me and I can't think of anything else. My heart's

FEAR OF THE MIND

racing as we begin dancing; the air around us was electric and my body had goosebumps all over. He's a gentleman when he dances and I follow his lead. Suddenly, he swoops me with both his hands and carries me in the direction of the basement. My eyes widen, not knowing what's happening. He's holding me close to his body and I can feel his breath mingle with mine as he walks down the staircase holding me in his arms.

He plops me down roughly against the old wall of the basement where water is cascading over the wall. The sudden chill of the water shocks the skin on my back but his hands are warm and his touch soothing. He then turns me softly to face a crack in the wall and the water flows all over me while he buries his face into my hair and kisses my neck. My nipples harden under the cold water cascade which has drenched my face and front, I feel his hands grab me in a tight embrace as he continues to kiss. He twists my hair roughly and pulls my head back toward him and swirls his tongue in my ears.

He lets go of my hair and turns me to face him again; I'm completely soaked wet and my bra and nipple is showing through my thin white tee. He rips apart my tee like he was freeing me from some invisible chains that held me captive. It's like I've been waiting for this all my life. I respond in kind and free him from his tee shirt, my fingers wander around his chest, touching and caressing him with my fingers. We're hungry for each other and no one can stop us tonight. He pulls my head up and kisses me passionately, our tongues swirling inside each other's mouth. He takes my clothes off and I'm so wet with desire. He licks and bites on my cookie and says, "You taste so sweet."

Then he inserts his penis inside me and if I had a rope I'd ride it like a bull in a rodeo straight to my G-Spot. He held my thighs and we rocked back and forth, thrusting his huge cock deep inside me. The pleasure was more than I could stand so I screamed, "Oh, I'm Cummmmming. Stop! Oh My God. Stop! I can't take anymore. Please, Stop!"

We made love as if we'd known every inch of each other's bodies like we'd done this a thousand times before in another lifetime. I look up to see his gorgeous eyes smile back at mine, and then rest my head on his chest as both of us lay exhausted, content and peaceful, like we were adrift in a bed of clouds. I soak in the warmth of his body and fall asleep.

As I sleep, there's that dream again, but this time I see a dark figure right in front of my eyes; his face is hidden from me but his hands are covering his chest. He moves away slowly from me and then uncovers his hands from the chest to reveal multiple stab wounds; there's blood all over him. I see him stumble and fall backward. My heart & mind is racing and I feel sweat trickle down my forehead. The putrid smell of blood is hitting my nose. I pry my eyes open to end this nightmare only to look down at a pair of blood stained hands. Those are my hands!! I wake up in panic and look around to see my mysterious guy, who I made love with, laying on the floor motionless, with multiple stab wounds in his chest!!!!

FEAR OF THE MIND

"No!!!!" I scream, my head spinning.

I feel his pulse, I bend low into his blood-ied chest to hear his heartbeat, nothing...he's dead!

I don't understand as my whole body be-gins to tremble over what's happened. All I remember is that he walked into my house for dinner and we made love here in the basement. I can't remember anything else until this nightmare happened; was it a nightmare or did it really happen? Why would I? How could I? My soul screams but my heart's gone deathly cold. There's blood all over the clothes that were strewn in yesterday's passionate heat.

I head upstairs, put on a robe and make a call 911. I cannot make sense of this. The first responders arrive, I'm breaking down unable to explain anything in a logical sense. I point them to the basement below to take the mystery guy's body that lay dead. They go downstairs when my business partner arrives; Eddie, puts a blanket around me and tries to calm me down, but I'm crying hysterically. I finally quiet down and recite everything I recall.

After ten minutes, the police come from the basement. I turn around, fully prepared to see the body of an adult male, 6ft 2 covered in white cloth and declared dead. Instead they have no body with them.

Eddie turns around, his eyes wide with concern says, "Martina, are you sure you're not on any medication or drinks? Did you consume alcohol or any type of drugs last evening?" Eddie asks, his voice gentle and soothing.

FEAR OF THE MIND

"Why would you ask me that? You know I don't do drugs. Eddie, where's his body? And yes, I did have two glasses of Moscato last night with him when we had dinner."

"Martina," Eddie whispers calmly, continuing, "You're not okay, I think you need to see a psychiatrist."

"What are you talking about?!" I scream.

"Are you saying I'm mental?"

"Martina, calm down, please!" Eddie says pacifying me. He looks on in horror and shock.

Eddie's gentle and kind face is contorted in worry and concern.

"Martina, I'm not sure you're ready to hear this, but the fact is, that the first responders' team, found no body there. They searched high and low, there's no body, no blood stains, nothing. Just a pair of jeans and a clean white tee."

I gape at him in shock hearing the words coming out of his mouth.

"Martina, you've not killed anyone, there's no one there. But you need professional help and possibly a long break from work." He says, placing his hand gently on my back.

"Tell me you're lying Eddie, what the heck is going on?! My hands were stained with blood, my clothes were stained with blood. He was lying there in a pool of blood." I cry, unable to fathom what was happening.

"Calm down sweetie, they're going to take you to the hospital and get you an appointment with a psychiatrist tomorrow.

"No, I'm not going to the hospital. I'm not sick. I just need to rest and then I blacked out. I don't remember how long I was blacked out then I hear a male voice say, "Martina, wake up."

"Martina" he whispers "open your eyes slowly now"

I do as directed and begin opening my eyes slowly to see the mysterious guy from my dream sitting in front of me in a white lab coat. I'm in a state of shock.

"Where am I? Who are you?" I say, panicking.

"Calm down Martina, you're doing absolutely fine. We play these mind games every Halloween." What was he talking about I see the stab wounds on his chest.

He said, "We're already dead, sweetie. We died five years ago in a car accident, and we come back as evil spirits to haunt this ungodly place. I'm beginning to hate it but this time around you really played your part, well. You scared the hell out of a lot of people this Halloween. Now give me your hand, it's time to go home."

What Were You Thinking

A friendly neighborhood with good folks for neighbors is a true blessing. Not mine! I feel like I've inherited a bunch of intellectually challenged dimwits for my neighbors. Who on earth paints a house mustard color, I have to wear my fucking sunglasses, it's shocking as hell like staring at the sun. I've thought of moving from here on more than one ocassion thanks to them. Meet Big Jim and his wife Kate, who looks nothing like the flower of the same name. Big Jim is over 6ft 4 tall, weighs at least 300 pounds and Kate his wife comes a close second, though is much shorter at 5ft 2. I don't like judging people based on their looks but when you've got no brains to match your physically imposing bodies, things take a comical turn. I've always been curious how they met and how their love story may have transpired because they've been pretty much the same through the last decade.

My name's Fred and I live here with my wife Linda and our dog, a chihuahua aptly named 'peanut' because of his diminutive size. My blood pressure is up looking at the latest antics of Big Jim. They've painted their house the brightest shade of mustard yellow they could find, it's like staring into the sun over the fence!

FEAR OF THE MIND

'Who on earth paints their house a mustard

yellow?!' I yell, for my wife to hear. She's getting changed into a bikini to sunbathe out on our poolside.

"Linda, you better cover yourself with a towel or something. I'm not going to stand around watching Big Jim oggling at your sexy body just because his wife can't fit into a thong!" I say to Linda, looking in the direction of our neighbors newly painted house. It's going to give me sore eyes.

Linda sashays in front of me wearing a powder blue bikini that shows off her gorgeous, lightly tanned body. She's voluptuous and sexy, a man's desire made flesh I say.

MARTHA PEREZ

I begin to calm down after I see her. I grab her and give her a deep kiss and smack her ass. She giggles, as she wears her sunglasses and holds her tanning lotion and a bathrobe and walks out to the poolside.

Big Jim once said to me over a couple of beers we were sharing on the 4th of July weekend, that Linda wasn't that great looking. He thought she's an attention seeker and that's the reason why she sunbathed ever so often to show off her curves in the hope that she'd get Jim's attention because he thinks that Linda fancies him. Jim boasted about his big dick and told me "Maybe you're a bit too small for her Fred" he said, laughing that obnoxious laugh of his. The nerve of this guy, I laughed it off. He's got a beer belly jiggling like jello. I get my Daisy Model straight shot BB gun. I aim and shoot his pitbull. The dog yells. Jim spits the cigar out of his mouth, not knowing why his dog is running around in circles crying. Yea, uh, huh. Don't mess with me, I mumble. I think the dog's name is 'Tiny'. Now who the hell names a pitbull 'Tiny'?!

Anyway, today I can see Big Jim puffing his cigar eyeing Linda from the distance.

"Asshole" I say out loud as I turn around to get myself a beer when I hear his voice shouting at me.

"Hey Fred, enjoying the day? It's a hot day ain't it?"

"Yea" I say, trying to rein in my temper.

"Hey, why don't you get a few beers and some chilli dogs and we'll get together on your poolside, it should be fun!" he says with a big grin.

My face reddens with anger and frustration , how do I avoid a freaking pool party with this guy. It's when I'm thinking of excuses that I see his wife Kate come out to their backyard with a plate of hot BBQ Peri peri chicken. It smells delicious and the aroma of it makes me salivate. If there's one thing Linda isn't good at, it's cooking which Kate has literally aced at. But seeing Kate in a pair of Daisy Dukes is nothing short of scary. I try to erase the thought of her dimpled thighs and legs and instead think of the fresh BBQ chicken they're roasting. Do I give into the temptation and call them over? I give in and motion with my hands for them to come over. Kate comes and gives me a big hug and hands me a plate of the spicy chicken legs and wings while Big

FEAR OF THE MIND

Jim hops over to Linda's tanning bed to say 'Hi'.

We talk about some routine stuff happening around our neighborhood; I see Jim's eyes are constantly on Linda, Kate also looks at her butt with envy. I tell Big Jim to help himself to some beer inside the kitchen as a way to give him a break from watching my wife. I go to Linda's side.

"Babe, put some clothes on, you don't want to be walking around in a bikini in front of Big Jim unless you want to make this friendly get together of sorts a very unfriendly one."

"What the hell Fred, can't a woman even tan at home in her own backyard? It's not my fault that men can't take their eyes off me, stop being such a prick," she said handing me her tanning lotion.

"Massage my back for me will you darlin?" she says with a coy smile.

"The favor will be returned tonight" she whispered as she winks at me shifting her sunglasses down.

"It's my favorite job in the world" I say, as I

start to rub her back and feel my hands over her tight ass, it's taste of what's to come later tonight and I was already excited.

Big Jim comes out with a dozen beers from our kitchen to see me massaging Linda's behind. I smile at him and quickly take a towel and cover her back. Kate comes over to Linda's tanning bed and the two start talking. I leave them to it and join Jim who's already on his fourth beer and sixth barbequed chicken leg. I take a bite of it, and admit it's pretty addictive. I could eat a whole bucket of it.

"It tastes fantastic Kate," I say raising my hand in acknowledgement to Kate, who smiles back.

"I can get you some more if you want, just let me know" she says as she looks to Linda.

"I'd love some Kate, I always hear so much about your fabulous cooking skills" Linda chimes in.

I'm beginning to relax when I see from the corner of my eye that 'Tiny' has crapped all over my lawn. I get up from my seat and go to take a closer look, stinks like hell I tell ya. I'm hopping mad in my head and almost want to take my BB gun and shoot the damn dog down. I don't see Jim coming from behind me but he puts his big arm around me.

"Don't mind that Fred, it's just dog poop, I'm sure Peanut does this just as often" he says trying to pacify me.

"Yea sure he poops, but we've trained Peanut to be as civilized as a dog can be, unlike Tiny." I say with frustration rising in my voice.

"Forgive him this time, don't make a fuss about it and spoil the fun today. You gotta relax a little Fred. You're always angry about something or the other".

He was right, I had to relax but who could relax with neighbors like him. Ugh. I mumble a "Yea" and walk back to the poolside, eager to have another beer.

We wrap up our little get together around noon time. I sigh in relief as they leave and look at Linda who now looks like a bronzed goddess, what a sight for sore eyes. I've eaten enough BBQ chicken and downed more than a couple of beers to get any action in bed right now, else I could've devoured my wife right now. I take my seat in the living room recliner and put my feet up from where I can clearly see her; her clean bikini line is peeking through her thongs and I feel myself get a hard on. She's bent over the kitchen sink getting the dishes done when she turns to look at me. She walks towards me and then gazes down.

"Seems like someone's in the mood for a massage," she quips and washes her hand. I can see her eyes sparkle with mischief. She heads over to the fridge and puts two small ice cubes in her mouth and comes close to me. She climbs atop me and I free her from whatever little threads are on her and feel her up as she goes down on me and gives me the most amazing sensation.

'I'm the luckiest guy on the planet' I think to myself as I see her blonde head bob around below between my crotch. She looks up at me, her mouth warm and moist with me and goes again. I'm in paradise.

We clean up and I doze off for a long nap. Linda is meeting some friend of hers for coffee so she tells and leaves around at 4pm.

It's around 6.30 pm and I decide to order food from Linda's favorite Mexican restaurant to surprise her. I place the order and sit on my Lazyboy chair and turn on the TV waiting for Linda and the dinner to arrive. I tune into one of my fave shows 'Three's Company', an oldie but agoodie; it makes me laugh everytime! It's

FEAR OF THE MIND

a good forty minutes later when I hear a loud noise. 'WTF was that?!' I say out loud and quickly go outside to see Big Jim's boat which has been hauled onto a trailer, squarely rammed into my 1979 Ford Mustang Classic!!!!

A few folks from other houses come out to see my now mangled car. Fuck, I'm going to kill that jiggle belly ass! I hear the door open and see Linda walk in.

"What happened Fred? You look a bit off, all good?" she says, concern etched all over her face. "Well you should see what happened to our beloved Mustang" I say, still looking at the car.

"Babe, call the cops, I'm going to whoop his ass," I say and angrily get out to meet Jim.

Jim hurries out to meet me as soon as he sees me heading over to his front porch.

"Sorry dude, it was lose. I had no idea" he says, in an apologetic tone.

"That's going to cost me a fortune and you a payback. I'm not letting you get away with this. First it was your dog, now it's your frickin boat."

I turn back to walk home when I turn back again to look at him.

"Expect the cops at your doorsteps".

I hear him stomp angrily and go back inside. He had this coming. I'm going to have call my insurance guys and check how much I can recover for this.

I get home hopping mad. Linda has neatly arranged dinner and is smiling in appreciation for ordering out from her favorite restaurant. She comes and hugs me.

FEAR OF THE MIND

"You're always thinking of me. It's so sweet of you to have ordered my favorite dishes from my favorite place. I love you Fred."

"I love you too hon" I say with a shrug, my mind still on the car.

"Oh and don't worry about the insurance, I just finished talking to the insurance company a few minutes ago and sorted it out with them. Everything's good" she says with a wide grin.

I sigh in relief. She motions me to sit down for dinner and we finish up our delicious meal of stuffed peppers, garlic & beef enchiladas and cocadas for dessert.

"Sweetie, why don't you go and shower, I'll clean up and join you in there soon" she says, grinning ear to ear.

I know she tries to relax me everytime she senses I'm tensed. She knows my temper flare ups more than anyone else. I wasn't going to leave her alone in the shower. But before that, there was something else to do.

"Linda honey, why don't you get me a towel from the kitchen, I need it to clean up the tool box in the basement, better to get dirty now and then take a shower."

Linda doesn't suspect anything. She heads to where our laundry is drying outside in our backyard while I pick up a big jar of crisco from the pantry and head out.

I go over to Big Jim's driveway tip toeing, careful not to make any sound or wake someone up. I carefully smear the driveway with crisco all over. How's that for payback. When I'm satisfied, I walk back the same way, quietly my body ready for some steamy action in the shower with my wife.

I get home to find Linda already waiting for me in the shower, her naked body wet. She puts her hands around me.

"Where did you disappear? I came with the cloth you were asking for but you weren't here" she said as she began kissing my neck.

"Just forgot something" I say with a chuckle as my hands wander eagerly to taste her and be inside her.

We spend close to an hour massaging each other's bodies with our tongues, hands, our faces and were buried in each other's juices before we cleaned up and went to sleep.

It's 7am when I hear loud screams coming from outside. Can't a man sleep here peacefully, ever?! I wake up butt naked and slip on a robe. I walk to the window to see a sight that had me burst with laughter.

There's Kate who's fallen down and is slipping across Jim's driveway, thanks to crisco which I had expertly smeared across the place. Poor Kate is drenched in crisco from head to toe, her curly hair slick with grease. Linda joins me from behind and suddenly grows concerned looking at Kate.

"What the hell happened to her Fred?" She says groggily.

"I don't know, looks like she took a fall in the driveway" I say smiling to myself.

"I hope nothing's happened to her" Linda says. We hear a knock on the door and Linda leaves to get it. When she leaves, I laugh softly so that she doesn't hear. I wouldn't want her to know that I was the one responsible for it.

FEAR OF THE MIND

I join Linda in the living room and find a cop standing in the hallway.

"This is my husband Fred, Fred this is officer Duncan" Linda says as she introduces us.

I extend my hand to the officer in a handshake and ask him to take a seat.

"Some coffee gentlemen?" Linda asks and the officer eyeing Linda, smiles in acknowledgement and looks at her as she excuses herself to the kitchen.

"We've received a complaint from your neighbor Jim that you're the one who's responsible for today morning's accidental fall of Jim's wife Kate. You have anything to say to that?"

"It's preposterous officer to think that I, of all the people would stoop to do something like that. I'm a respected man and I have no reason to do something like that to his wife when I'm quite happy with my own. No offense officer, but they're known to be an annoying bunch by many in our neighborhood, you can ask a few of them if you like."

Linda walks in with the coffee and the officer's attention is completely on her. He takes the coffee from her and smiles at her like a high school kid who's just hit the jackpot.

"Is there anything to worry about officer?" Linda says with a seductive smile.

"Oh no, nothing at all. This is just routine because we received a complaint. Thankfully, Kate hasn't suffered from any injuries or anything, else the case would've been subject to a serious investigation. Great coffee by the way," the officer says.

"Oh that's such a relief to hear" Linda says.

"Thank you officer, I'm glad there's no trouble."

The officer stands up, flashes a big smile to Linda while I roll my eyes. I walk him to the door and see him off.

It's about an hour later that I hear Jim calling my name outside. I head in the direction of his voice, it's coming from his backyard. I go to our poolside.

"We're not friends anymore you loser," he yells.

"Haven't I brought you coffee & donuts whenever you've felt low Fred? Why did you do this?"

"I don't know what you're talking about Jim, you're hurting my feelings by talking like this. I'm glad nothing happened to Kate, you should be grateful."

"You jerk, I know it's you who smeared crisco in the driveway, only you could come up with something like that. You warned me about a payback just didn't see it coming like this!"

"What? Jim, we've been friends since your wife weighed 110 pounds, our friendship has grown with each pound she's put on, about 200 odd since. Don't hurt me by talking like this" I say and show him my middle finger and walk back to the house as he continues to shout some choice words for me.

I close the door behind me, feeling nothing.

FEAR OF THE MIND

It's the next day that I see that Jim is setting up surveillance cameras all around his property and backyard. This angers me as I couldn't mess around anymore because I'll be caught red handed if I did something. I decide to take my BB gun and shoot down the cameras. Kate and their dog Tiny are in the backyard with a couple of budweisers and a tray of nachos & dips, waiting on Jim to join them.

I look at my damaged Mustang and a tear rolls down my cheeks; it was my first car and my favorite among the 3 cars I own. I'm sensitive about things I've bought with my hard earned cash just like anyone else. I wait for Jim, Kate and their dog to head out so that I can shoot every one of those stupid cameras down. After about two hours, they head out as expected. Linda has gone out to meet her friend and will be back for lunch after which she wants us to go shopping.

I take my BB gun and shoot from my poolside aiming at the cameras I can see. I feel satisfied as a punk and run a few errands. Linda comes home lunch in hand–some fish & chips, chicken burritos and green salad. I look at Linda, she's dressed in a body hugging deep beige, knee length dress. It suits her to the T. She was glowing with each passing day and I remarked this to her.

"You're the only reason for this glow" she quips smiling at me.

"Well we've been having more fun, don't ya think?" I say with a chuckle.

"You're my sexy beast" she teases. We finish lunch and though I'm in no mood to head out shopping, she drags me by hand. I would've spend the whole afternoon banging her but she wants me to pick out some lingerie for her. Well, at least it's not boring. I get to choose what color and what patterned thongs and bras she wants to wear before I can tear them off her. I'd do this for free I think to myself.

Linda drives to her favorite place for lingerie shopping. The guy at the shop is eyeing Linda and flashes a nasty smile. I turn up beside her and take a seat as we start going through tiny pieces of cloth that's going to caress my wife's butt and breasts. I look at Linda and whisper in her ears.

"You're forty years old, so deal with it. You're not wearing this stuff out, just for me in our bedroom." I say tightening my grip on her shapely ass.

"We'll see," she says ignoring me.

I pinch her and then put my hand between her thighs to feel her juicy bits.

"Stop making me horny here Fred," she whispers in my ears.

We finish shopping and stop for some refreshments before heading home.

When we arrive home, Linda tries out all her new lingerie in front of me as I lay on the bed, telling her which one's were my favorites. She looks hot in anything she wears so it wasn't very hard to choose. There's an animal print set in there which looks particularly stunning on her. It's when she goes to change into another pair of lingerie that I suddenly hear sounds of Tiny and Peanut coming from the poolside. Linda hears it too and hurries out of the closet with a robe on.

"What the hell is going on?" she says, panicking.

"Lets go and have a look babe," I say, swiftly getting up from the bed and putting on some pyjamas.

We hurry to where the sounds were coming from. When we arrive on the poolside, we see Peanut laying on the floor motionless with blood around him. Tiny, Jim's pitbull is barking aggressively, his bloodied teeth proof of crime. He bit Peanut. Linda bends down to pick up Peanut, horrified and distraught. I'm shocked and mad, a sudden rage comes over me. I head back inside and take my BB gun and point it at Tiny. I keep shooting multiple times till he's as dead as he possibly can be. I'm crying hysterically having lost Peanut and shooting Tiny. Jim comes running out and screams "No...!!!!!!!" That was the end of everything bet-

ween us.

Jim and Kate soon moved out and put the house on sale. I got a two year jail term in the midst of which Linda filed for divorce. She cleaned up all my savings, took my home and a car. Last heard, she was having two affairs, one with the guy at the lingerie shop and officer Duncan. I didn't think I'd lose her, always thought I was the luckiest man around. Now I'm out of jail and homeless. I spend my time doing odd jobs and spend whatever little I earn on getting drunk. No maintainence, no mortgage, no bills, don't even have to take a bath because there's no woman to make me

FEAR OF THE MIND

feel like a King. My buddies are those I made
in jail, we play cards together and roam the
streets looking for scraps. What was I thinking?
I lose everything for shooting a dog dead.
Where I came from, it's called an eye for an
eye, a tooth for a tooth. But there's a heavy
price to pay for that and though I've no
attachments or possessions of my own now,
I'm   at   peace.

Dark Mountain

Maya, wake up sleepy head! We have to get ready for our trip to the cabin. You don't want to keep your parents waiting now, do you, sweetheart?"

I hear my husband Kenny say as I hear his footsteps hustling around to pack our bag for a week of vacay at a mountaintop cabin. I sense his voice bursting with excitement and rightly so. I've been looking forward to this trip since the last few months. I just gave birth to our son Levi five months ago and haven't had a wink of sleep or the time to relax. The struggle of motherhood is real, not that I regret it! I wouldn't trade it for anything in the world but boy, could I do with some sleep and some time away. We plan to leave Levi with my parents for the week; they've been dying to see him.

I'm still in bed, half asleep and turn to read the clock on my bedside table, it's about 6.40am. Levi is still fast asleep, thankfully but knowing his routine, I know he'd be up within the hour.

Kenny climbs from beneath the bed covers and surprises me with kisses all along my inner thighs, his fingers caress my most intimate parts and then I feel his tongue swirl inside, as I tug and pull his hair as his head is buried inside my moist and creamy muffin. He tongues me deeply as I moan and writhe in pleasure. Oh I have missed this. I want him so bad inside me. He lifts his head and says "Come to Daddy" as he hoists himself directly above me and sucks my breasts; I can feel him devouring my breast milk which is beginning to trickle down my abdomen and into my belly button. Kenny goes down the trail and sucks my belly button and all the way back, while still playing with his fingers inside me, the sensation is delicious.

I try to pry his head off my breasts as I say "Save some for our son will you?"

He laughs "Yes Ma'am" and then kisses me. I push him aside teasingly.

"We have a whole week to ourselves, so this will have to wait," I say winking at him and getting up from bed. I have to get a couple of bottles prepped for Levi and pack some of his stuff.

I walk around in my bathrobe, multitasking. I'm brushing and packing the bag. I hear Levi waking up with a yawn and then he bawls, a sound the house has become accustomed to ever since his arrival. I finish up and hurry to feed him as Kenny wraps around the rest of the packing.

"Maya, should we take all the blankets?" Kenny asks as he holds up three of our coziest winter quilts.

"I think we should just take one. It's only a couple of hours away besides, it's just the two of us," I say giving him a mischievous smile, it's been awhile since I felt anything remotely sexy.

"Okay sweetheart, if you say so," he responds back, acknowledging my dirty intent.

We dress up and get ready to go. I've worn a black turtleneck full sleeve top, a pair of steel grey chequered trousers, some black ankle length boots and a charcoal grey long coat. I feel good looking at myself in the mirror. Post partum has been hard enough; I don't remember the last time I actually dressed up. I dab on some cherry lip balm and put my freshly tousled hair into a low loose chignon, which is my go-to mommy hairstyle. Levi is calm but awake after his feed; I'm hoping he's lulled into sleep again on our way to my parent's house. Kenny loads up our Range Rover with our baggage and straps Levi's baby seat in the car's backseat.

FEAR OF THE MIND

Kenny starts the car and we're on our way. My parent's house is just an hour away from where we live and the route was relatively hassle-free. Since we had an early start, we hope to make it in under an hour because there isn't much traffic. Since neither Kenny nor I had any breakfast, we decide to stop at a drive through and pick up some pulled pork sandwiches, fried chicken, French onion soup, two large fries and a mug of hot chocolate for me. Bliss! Kenny passes on the steaming hot brown bags with our order. I'm eager to dig in and take out two of the sandwiches which smell heavenly. I pass one to Kenny as he begins to munch as he drives.

I'm feeling so happy and relaxed, it's been awhile. Kenny and I start humming one of our favorite tunes, 'You are my sunshine, my only sunshine, you make me happy even when the skies are grey'. I turn back to Levi smiling looking out the window, seemingly enjoying the snowy scenery. The trees are under a blanket of snow and the scenery reminds me of a Thomas Kinkade painting.

"Did you hear that the lady across the street is getting lots of male visitors?" I ask looking at Kenny.

"I really think she's selling drugs or something, that's what most of our neighbors are saying. I avoid that area when I take Levi out for his stroll," I continue.

"Never a dull moment on our block," Kenny says with a smile and then leans to kiss my cheeks.

"I love you babe, I know it's been hard for you dealing with post partum but I'm so proud of you. You know you're doing great. Seeing you with Levi transitioning into this new role of being a Mom, has made my heart swell with love and respect for you." Kenny says.

"Awe, I love you too. You know I wouldn't have been able to do this without you Kenny. You're being a great dad to Levi and have always been the wind beneath my wings." I say, my eyes welling up with emotion.

"I don't know if it's motherhood or what but I get so emotional these days for everything," I say laughingly as I wipe my eyes with a tissue.

"You're doing just fine, I love you, don't ever forget that," Kenny says.

Kenny continues to drive as I fall asleep. It's 35 minutes into the drive when I suddenly feel the car screeching and wake up.

MARTHA PEREZ

We were on a narrow road with valley on one side and rocky hills on another. There was a truck that cornered us to the narrow end of the road, a little too close for comfort. I see a deer hop right in front of us and scream at Kenny, 'Brakes!' He tried to and then lost control of the vehicle, like the brakes weren't working! The Range Rover was veering left out of control, going over a cliff and diving into the valley below. It wasn't a very deep valley but it's hard to think anyone would survive a fall from here. We scream as we crash headlong, all I could think was of Levi. My life up until now flashed before me like a film as if it was all going to end. I close my eyes as I feel our car hit the ground. I was knocked out by the impact, unaware of whether I was dead or alive. I didn't feel any movement, there was only darkness.

I pry my eyes open suddenly, breathing heavily. I see the car's airbags on the front and sides inflate against my body which is still strapped to the seat. I turn to see Kenny on my side, bleeding from his head, resting on the steering wheel. My mind panics as I think of my baby and try turning behind to see Levi but I wince in pain as I'm unable to turn to my right; the abdomen and my legs hurt. The whole right side of my body feels nothing, like it's gone numb. I adjust the rearview mirror to see Levi still safe and attached to his car seat. I can tell he's been crying because his face is red and his eyes are watery. I want to hold my baby but we need to get out first.

MARTHA PEREZ

"Kenny! Kenny! Honey wake up please!" I say shaking Kenny with whatever little strength is left in me. He's not responding to me, it's like he's fallen unconscious on impact. I start crying, unable to think. I try calling 911 through our cars radio system but everything's been shattered and is lying around in pieces. My face has small broken pieces of glass pricking it and so does Kenny. I panic and feel my blood pressure rise; I feel dizzy and see blackness come over my eyes. I faint. I don't know how many hours have passed when I hear Levi's crying pierce through to my ears. I wake up. My poor baby, I'm not even able to hold him or move from here. I try talking to Levi, in a vain attempt to pacify him. We were literally in the middle of nowhere.

I suddenly hear Kenny's voice beside me.

FEAR OF THE MIND

"Maya?"

"OMG, you're alive. I thought I'd lost you there." I say crying and trying to hug Kenny. He lifts his head, I tell him to be careful.

He motions with his hand that's he's alright.

"Kenny, I need to hold Levi, can you please try to unstrap him from his seat?"

"Wait a sec, let me try." He says as he reaches behind and removes the straps holding Levi. I watch him do this adjusting the rearview mirror. After an agonizing few minutes, he manages to lift Levi up and puts him in my lap.

"Oh my precious, you're okay." I say examining his little hands and feet, there's not a scratch on him.

"May be your guardian angels were protecting you," I say as I plant kisses on his beautiful face.

We've been stuck here for more than six hours and have been trying to just open the car doors. After many unsuccessful attempts and spending the last of our energy on it, I tell Kenny to rest up and wait for help to arrive. I'm sure someone, anyone, will spot us or start looking for us.

Daylight was dimming and the sun was beginning to get low early as is the case during winters. The temps will fall below zero out here in no time. I urge Kenny to pull out the sole blanket we'd carried, instantly regretting the decision to pack only one. Kenny and I huddle together in the blanket, holding Levi close to my chest to keep him warm.

FEAR OF THE MIND

Two days passed by and there's been no help in sight. We've been freezing under the weather and only yesterday night did we have some respite from the snow fall. Our car is buried a feet and half in snow, lying at the foot of the valley. I was hoping that my parents who were expecting us would've informed the cops and started a search & rescue by now. Desperation was creeping into my mind, Kenny's bleeding stopped but he often feels disoriented and sees things in a blur, it keeps happening sporadically and was worrying. Little Levi was the only reason I was fighting to stay alive against all odds.

"Maya" Kenny said reading my thoughts. I turn to face him. I see his face etched in worry.

"I'm going to go and find some help. We cannot sit here and wait for help to come, its tough luck. I'll go up the mountain tomorrow and get some help; I'm thinking I'll set out by sunrise."

"You can't be going alone and leaving us here. Not with that head injury Kenny, no way." I protest.

"Look, if we wait here, you're going to run out of nourishment to produce any milk to feed Levi, he's just 5 months old, not a fully grown adult. He cannot survive in such harsh weather for another day. I have to take this chance else
we're going to die out here."

I start to cry, overwhelmed by the gravity of the ordeal we're in. Kenny was right; Levi is too small to survive these conditions without food and enough warmth. For the time being, my body could keep him warm but for how long? My right rib seems like it has a fracture and I find it challenging to move even a little bit, I bite my lower lip to keep calm when the pain becomes too much.

"Maya, if I don't return in two days time, you're going to have to take Levi and make the trek. Let's hope it doesn't come to that. I love you both." Kenny says, tears welling up in his eyes.

Sleep didn't come that night. My mind was sick with worry about Kenny's impending trek up the mountain; this wasn't familiar territory. All he was going to have with him is a flashlight and his jacket. Wolves and other animals are known to roam these mountains. I was terrified by the mere thought of it. I spent the night cradling Levi to sleep while watching Kenny asleep on my side. Somewhere along the dark, cold night, I fell asleep out of exhaustion.

I wake up the next morning with Levi's cry; he's hungry. I feed him and strap him to myself. The sun was beginning to rise on the horizon and the sky was turning a pale golden pink. Kenny and I exchange only fleeting glances as I pack a 200ml tetra pack of juice, a mini bottle of water and a bag of chips. The silence between us was deafening because we didn't know if we'd see each other again.

Kenny kisses Levi on his little head bundled in a hoodie and then turns to give me a deep, long kiss. It was heartbreaking, tears running down our cheeks. He takes the bag from me and struggles to get out through the car door which is jammed. He hands me back the bag and instead steps out of the car through the window, which has no glass left.

He looks through the window at me and Levi.

"Maya I've never loved anyone as I've loved you and Levi. I will do so till my dying breath."

"Promise me you'll look after yourself Kenny, be careful out there. I love you and I know you'll be back to take us." I say, crying.

We hold hands and then he turns around to navigate the nooks and crevices of this mountain that lay ahead of him; I'd be waiting here on a wing and a prayer, hoping to see him alive and coming back with help. Kenny slowly disappears from sight into the whiteness of the cold valley.

MARTHA PEREZ

I'm holding onto Levi for dear life, on the edge of my sanity. There's a strong cold wind blowing taking snow with it and the landscape slowly shifts before my eyes bringing more snow with it. The cloudless sky was turning a deep golden and red, indicating nightfall was close at hand. It was colder than the last two days. I wrap the blanket even more tightly around Levi and me; this was going to be a long hard night. I stay alert through the night as I heard howling intermittently from a distance. It scared me to death and I tried to lay low with Levi, the inflated air bag on the side was my only cushion between the shattered window glass and the chilly air outside. I managed to squeeze in one of our big bags through the broken window on the side of the driver's seat to keep the cold air outside from coming in.

I was restless through the night thinking about Kenny, where was he? Did he find help, did he reach the top? Did he eat something? These thoughts kept racing through my mind. I didn't sleep and was awake to see the sun rise on another new day. I thought to myself, how lucky I'd considered myself to be, for having a husband who loves me as much as Kenny does, and now to have a beautiful son like Levi. Life has thrown a pitchfork in my way and I was determined to overcome it. I have to fight for my son and for myself, hoping that Kenny would've made it.

It's very windy today; I feed Levi with the bottles I'd prepared for him before we left and I eat sparingly from one of the sandwiches we'd brought from our drive through order. I had to conserve my food. I was feeling anxious as Kenny is supposed to be heading our way by tonight. He said if I didn't see him today also, I'd have to take Levi and go. Little Levi, oblivious to what's happening, looks up at me and presses his little nose and mouth against my face; I hug him with all my might, my little bundle of joy. My nerves were tense and my mind restless as dusk was giving way to night. I had to think of getting out with Levi by tomorrow morning. I held onto Levi and slept through the night.

It's around 4am when I'm woken up by a dream of Kenny telling me to leave before sunrise. My heart's feeling uneasy about the dream, a feeling that something has happened to Kenny. I start crying, feeling overwhelmed by the situation I'm in. I look at Levi who's peacefully asleep over my left shoulder.

I start making a bag with Levi's bottles; only two are remaining of the four I'd prepared for him. I eat the remaining half of the sandwich I'd saved yesterday and pack a piece of fried chicken and a pack of the large fries we'd ordered for my trek. The clock on the car dashboard read 5.20am. I remove the inflated air bag from the side and try to get out. The car door is jammed on my side as well, so the only way to step out was the window. I remove shards of glass from its pane. Levi is firmly strapped to me but my one hand is covering him over my chest. I use my free hand to get a grip on the roof of the car while I hoist myself to the bottom of the window pane. I stick one leg out onto the ground below me and wince out in pain. The right side below my breast is hurting so bad that I feel dizzy. I collapse onto the snow below holding onto Levi and start crying. How was I to make a trek up a mountain like this I had no clue. I look at my baby's face. He's wide awake now but he isn't making any sound. He's got a dusting of snow on his little powder blue colored hoodie; as I brush it off, he gives a little sneeze. I smile and cry again, I need him and want him. I was determined to make it out of here alive.

I try standing up, still in pain and wrap the thick blanket around Levi and me. Using a ski board that Kenny had loaded into our car behind; I place the bag and a few of our belongings and tie it with a rope. It's freezing cold and my face was bearing the full brunt of the wind that's not chapped my face red. I drag the ski board with one hand with my other hand over Levi and start walking. My boots were sinking in the snow and each step I was taking was heavy and difficult, the pain near my rib cage was getting worse. I keep walking till I see the sun beginning to set over the horizon. There's a narrow rocky hollow a few meters from where I could take shelter for the night. I was petrified of sleeping outdoors but the hollow would camouflage against the white snowy landscape. I carefully step down to examine, it's about 4 ft deep, 3 ft wide and 8ft long, a crevice in the ground. I bundle up in the narrowest part of the hollow, covering myself and Levi from head to toe with the blanket. I pray that we survive this night and no animals spot us. It's dark now and the only sound that I can hear is of Levi and my breathing, and the howling of the wind.

When the wind calms down, I lift the blanket a little and look above. I'm struck by the beauty of the nighttime sky which is like a shroud of twinkling stars and silver moon light. In that moment, I felt like I was not alone, that someone was watching us.

I wake up with sunlight warming my face. I looked down at Levi who was still asleep; we had made it through a night. I take my food bag strapped to the ski board and pull out something to eat. I kept one of Levi's bottles in my long coat. It looked like it was around 8 or 9am, I could cover much ground during the day and would have to find a place before the sun dips low. My leg was feeling better but my toes weren't and neither were my fingers. I

FEAR OF THE MIND

wasn't feeling much there and I tried to warm them up. My ribs were still hurting but I had no time to dwell on the pain. This was life or death. Four days went by, hiding in crevices and caves by night and walking around in circles during the day. I wasn't getting anywhere and my legs were hurting and freezing. They were also beginning to ache and the pain was numbing. I decide to sit on a rock and take off my boots and socks. I scream in horror as I see all my toes go black. I hurriedly take off my gloves too. I begin to cry as I see my fingers looked the same deathly black and blue. Levi starts bawling seeing me cry and I try to stay calm. I put back on my gloves, socks and boots. I look into the vast emptiness before me and whisper a silent prayer. Help me and my son or just let us die out here, I can't take it anymore.

I walk, ignoring the pain in my feet, fingers and ribs, holding Levi and dragging our little ski board. After about 4 hours or so, around noontime when the sun was beginning to almost blaze down from above my head, I see an empty cave like hollow in the rocks. I drag my feet with whatever little energy is left of me and push myself to reach the cave. I look at Levi whose beautiful green eyes are focused on me. I kiss him gently and say "Mommy's tired, we should get some sleep, shouldn't we?" saying this I fall asleep holding on tightly to my baby.

I had another dream of Kenny. He whispered in my ears, "Help is on the way

FEAR OF THE MIND

Maya, hold on, you and Levi are going to be okay. I love you".

I wake up feeling a sense of calm and relief but I'm unable to move my feet. This sets off panic in my mind, I still have some movement in my hands and fingers but my legs are stiff with pain and so is my ribcage. I close my eyes breathing heavily, unsure of whether I'd make it out of here alive. There's no food left and I scoop some snow to put in my mouth, it stings my lips which are chapped dry. After a few hours as twilight comes, I notice something. Levi's breathing has slowed. I try to wake him up. He's asleep but his breathing sounds heavy, like he's struggling to breathe. I check his hands & feet and rub them to warm them up. He hasn't cried the whole day for his feed either, something was off. The last thing I need is thoughts of losing him because there'd be absolutely nothing worth fighting for.

We spend two days in the cave; I'm beginning to slip in and out of consciousness like it's my last. I can feel a pall of darkness come over me. Levi hasn't moved much but I can feel his little breath on my neck as he lies on my shoulder. I whisper 'Please keep my baby alive, please' and drift out of consciousness again.

I don't know whether it's night or day. I'm awake but I have no strength to get up and my feet have failed me, because they're not moving. I hear noises in the distance and think I'm hallucinating. I almost black out when I feel two strong hands lift me, after that I don't remember anything.

FEAR OF THE MIND

I wake up to a white ceiling above me and nurses hovering around me and what looks like an incubator to my left. My vision is blurry so I close my eyes again and open them. I'm in the hospital and Levi is placed in the incubator. The nurse motions to another nurse to inform the doctor. I hear her saying, "She's conscious, get Dr.Kuhlman in and inform her parents"

The nurse then walks to my side.

"Hello sweetie, the doctor will be here to see you. Don't say anything right now, you need to rest." She says smilling.

"How's my baby doing?" I ask, tears rolling down my cheek.

"He's a fighter just like his Mom. He's stable and is taking in food," she replied motioning her hands to his incubator.

"You've done well to hold him close to your body Maya, it's a miracle you both have survived in such harsh conditions" she says.

"How many days was I out like that?" I ask.

"About four nights and five days; you arrived at the hospital the day before yesterday."

I see my parents come to my room.

The nurse continues. "Unfortunately, we weren't able to save your fingers and toes. They had severe frostbite and were beyond repair. We've had to amputate them before the gangrene could do more damage." She says with a sympathetic face.

I try to look below at my feet bandaged in white strips with no toes and then hold my hands in front of my face. Three of my fingers on my right hand have been cut, my thumb and pointed finger remain; on the left hand, my ring finger, middle finger and thumb remain, the other two were cut off.

I start crying and my Dad and Mom hold me together, trying to pacify me as best as they can. I push them away, panicking and thinking about Kenny.

"How's Kenny?" I ask.

They look at each other, in silence. Dad speaks up.

"Kenny didn't make it Maya. He was attacked by a mountain lion. I'm sorry" he said, his face contorted in pain over my fate.

"No!!!!!!!!!!!!!" I scream over and over again. I'm unable to bear this much pain, the nurses hold me down and give me a shot to make me sleep.

It's been four years since the horrific accident happened and changed my life forever. We never made it to the cabin and I lost Kenny. I now fight for people with disabilities and work as an activist while holding a full time job as an office clerk. Levi had a speedy recovery and was discharged from the hospital before me; he was well loved by the nurses and doctors during his stay at the hospital. I go for physical therapy every couple of weeks to regain strength in my limbs. I met a wonderful man two years ago when I was in rehabilitation therapy. We married last February after a two year relationship. Levi was now four years and six months old, he was the ring bearer at our wedding. I'd never thought I'd find love again after losing Kenny, it was unthinkable. But life always gives us a reason to live on. Kenny's spirit lived on through Levi, in his green eyes, in his little tantrums and his love for peanut butter & jelly sandwiches just like his father. He'll always be a part of my life and my heart as his memories live on. C'est la vie Such is life.

A Brother's Betrayal

I wake up in the arms of my gorgeous fiancé Keith. He has a deep set of green eyes and lavish lips that arouse my senses. I want to make love to him so badly; I'm dying with anticipation. My heart is pumping blood through my veins like a fast-moving river eager to meet the sea. He kisses and licks my neck making my whole-body shiver with delight. Then he puts his body on top of mine, covering it like a warm blanket. His tongue travels down my stomach and circles my naval and finds my lace black panties. He places soft kisses on and around my cookie. Oh my god, the sweet sensations; I can't wait for my treat; the anticipation is making me so wet. Keith is the only man that I've felt this way for, the man I want to spend the rest of my life with. He puts his fingers inside my panties just enough for me to feel the tip of his fingers on my clitoris–making me want to guide his hand. Then he stops and says, "Sorry babe you will have to wait until tonight."

"Baby you can't leave me like this, please baby my pussy is so wet. Don't you hear it calling out your name?

"Yes, but I want you to think about it all day. I want you bursting from the seams to-night." Plus, I have to get back to work. That was just a little foreplay before the main show."

Keith likes making me wait so that sex can be intense. I'll be really horny by the time he comes home. He is picking up his brother Mike from the airport. He says his brother was always the bad boy and loved women and left them as he pleased. Keith says Mike wants to start a business as a mechanic. I've never met him and don't know anything about him. I'll soon find out as Keith was thinking of taking Mike to dinner at this little place called, "'Shake it up'." The place always had a lot of women looking for one-night stands or whatever they can put their hands on. Keith was busy, so he asked me to meet him at the restaurant. I'm wearing some tight jeans and a blouse that shows the outline of my nipples.

FEAR OF THE MIND

I'm wearing 6-inch heels and my black hair is lightly curled. I keep my makeup light with lots of mascara, long eyelashes & a nude-pink lip gloss. Keith loves when I dress like this because it draws plenty of attention and makes all the women stare at him, but he only has eyes for me. I see him at the bar, so I walk over to him swaying my hips; I want to tease him for leaving me so horny. I wanted him to know you can't leave me in the ocean and don't expect the sharks to bite. We kiss, and he presses my body to him, and I could feel his penis rise.

He whispers in my ear, "Are you thinking about sex and how good it will be when I get you home?"

Goodness gracious, he was reading my mind. "Oh yes! I am." I say whispering into his ear. He's wearing a white shirt showing his muscles, black slacks, and his hair slicked back. Goodness. I want him badly enough to make love right now.

We take a table and I order a glass of white wine and Keith gets a scotch on the rocks. I ask Keith where his brother Mike was, he said he went to the restroom. Then I see a guy walk toward us with a big smile. He had a confident walk and swagger about him. He was tall, tanned, and handsome.

Keith gets up and hugs him. I couldn't take my eyes off of him. "This is my girlfriend, Lena Waters. Lena, this is my brother Mike."

Mike said, "Well you never told me how beautiful she is. She looks like a model."

I said, "I'm hardly a model. But thanks for the compliment." We laughed.

FEAR OF THE MIND

Keith and Mike talked, catching up on things. Keith and I danced, drank and had a good time   I noticed that Mike couldn't stop staring at me.

The DJ announced on the microphone the last call for alcohol; that was our cue to leave and get ahead of the crowd who would certainly go to 'Jakes' for breakfast. The restaurant is famous worldwide for its delicious pancakes and fried chicken wings.   Afterward, we dropped Mike at his hotel where he had a business meeting in the morning.

Keith took me home, and he couldn't wait to get his hands on me. We lay on the bed and were like animals kissing and touching every inch of each other's bodies.

Keith whispered, "You are so hot baby then rips my panties with his teeth. He starts to lick my cookie, and I put it closer to his mouth. He says, "Don't stop moving baby. I like it when you move your hips." Omg, that just made me move even more. I came over and over again. I was so weak I couldn't feel my legs. Sweat was dripping from my body and my pussy was soaking wet. After we made love, I fell fast asleep in Keith's arms. I had a strange dream about Keith's brother, Mike that I'm too embarrassed to tell anyone about. I woke up and looked over to make sure that is was Keith lying next to me and not Mike.

The next morning Keith says, "I forgot to give Mike some money, and I have an important meeting. Could you take it for me?"

Apparently, Mike had just leased a place in town. I was feeling guilty about the dream and wished he didn't ask me that. "Do I have to?"

"He's soon to be your brother in law Lena. Do me that favor."

"All right, I'll drop it off on my way to my hair appointment." Later, I shower and put on a pair of blue jeans, a tie-up white blouse, and some sexy black strappy heels. I grab the keys to my red convertible Mazda MX and drive across town.

"Hi, Mike."

"Hello, Lena! Nice seeing you again. You are a sight for sore eyes." He says with a big smile.

I said yeah okay, "Here's the money that your brother sent you."

He gave me a sexy smile and the next thing I knew, I'm against the wall and Mike is touching my ass. He kisses my neck, and I didn't want him to stop. Then he blurted out,

"I wanted you the first time I saw you, and I could feel that you wanted me too. I can give you more than my brother could ever give you." He said, boring his green eyes into mine.

Right then, I had this overwhelming desire that I wanted to taste his manhood. I've never felt this way before. I unfastened his belt and pulled out his big, thick cock. I fall on my knees; it was pure madness. He tastes like sugar and spice, everything just right. My tongue could do wonders; my lust was out of this world. He says, "Oh baby you suck like no other. Come here, don't make me come. He lifts me from the floor and removes my jeans and panties and unties my blouse. He inserts his dick inside me inch by inch and says, "Your so wet and so tight. I holler, "OH GOD PLEASE!!" I wrap my legs around him his waist, and he pounds my pussy. The moves were rough but good. He was driving me out of my mind. We both exploded with ecstacy.

I breathe deeply to catch my breath and I hurry to put on my panties and jeans. I was feeling guilty about what I did. I had spontaneous sex with Keith's brother, "oh my God" I say to myself feeling embarrassed over what just transpired. What have I done?! I say under my breath. I turned around to face Mike. I said, "We had a connection last night I dreamt of you, but he's your brother Mike. I've been with him for awhile and we are engaged. For god sakes, he will never forgive us if he finds out."

He said, "Oh don't worry, he will never find out. I wanted you the moment I laid eyes on you."

"No this is not right, I will not be between you both. I love Keith, too much."

He looked into my eyes and said, "If you loved my brother, you never would have had the hottest sex you just ever had. As you can see, I'm much better than my brother, that's for sure." He said cockily.

What have I got myself in to? Mike doesn't give a shit about his brother. I knew that it would be trouble and it would never be the same with Keith again.

Mike said, "You will crave for me and dream about me constantly. You will only have eyes for me."

I said, "Get out of my way, you jerk."

"Yea, you know I'm telling you the truth. You were begging me not to stop."

FEAR OF THE MIND

Mike is laughing at me–I'm so angry, I walk out and slam the door. I could still hear his laughter. Keith calls my cell phone to see if I delivered the money. I told him yes. It was shocking what I did to Keith. I fucked his brother. I feel like a slut. How will I be able to stare into his eyes and make love to him? I will never forgive myself. I'm a low down unfaithful bitch, I really am. Is this what I've become?!

I get home and quickly strip down and take a shower. I smell him all over my body and taste him in my mouth. I brush my teeth a hundred times and gargle.

I'm supposed to meet Keith for dinner at 'Jenllanos' an Italian restaurant. I don't know how I can cover up my guilt. I'm sure it's written all over my face. Maybe I should tell

Keith that I slept with his brother. Karma is a bitch, and one day he will probably find out anyway.

When I walk in, my eyes widen in shock. Mike is sitting at the table with Keith. He didn't tell me he was going to be here. "Hey baby," Keith says, "I hope you didn't mind if Mike joined us this evening. He felt lonely so, I invited him to come." What the fuck is going on here, why am I put into this situation? I say to myself, trying to contain my anger.

"Hi Lena give me some love," Mike says with a smile.

Keith said, "Yeah, Lena give my brother some love."

I reluctantly hugged Mike.

Keith cleared his throat to speak. 'So what's been going on bro."

FEAR OF THE MIND

"Not much I met, this wild hungry woman, a sex goddess of a girl," Mike said with a mischievous grin and then looks at me. I go dead face.

"Wow, really you just got here and you found someone like that? Boy, you work fast. Mike, you should get your business established first before you get into a relationship, you know?"

"I will Keith, but I like to have a warm body in my bed."

Then Mike started to feel my leg under the table. What nerve, I moved his hand and said, "Please, excuse me I have to go to the ladies room." I wiggle my way out of this embarrassing situation and don't return till the boys have ordered dessert. I tell Keith that I'm unwell and tell him to hurry along dinner as I wanted to go home and rest. Little did Keith know about the guilt wallowing in my mind and body. Mike's presence was uncomfortable beyond words could say.

Weeks passed, and I kept thinking about the night that we made love. Mike was right; I was feining for him like a drug. I showed up one night at Mike's place when Keith was out for business. When he opened the door, he didn't look surprised. Instead he said, "I knew one day, you would come back to me."

" I said, "I couldn't resist.'

"Lena, what do you want me to do tonight?"

"I want you to eat my pussy until I tell you to stop–I should never have told him that. OMG, he did it so good that I was hooked from then on. It was like he had a special way of doing it. I never had a man do it like that before.

I stopped making love to Keith and didn't want him to touch me anymore. Our relationship was going down a slippery slope. I traded the man I loved for lusty, dirty, passionate sex with a manwhore who was his brother. I was addicted, and there was nothing I could do about it.

One cold and dreary day, I went over to Mike's house. I didn't know Keith had followed me. Mike and I were in the middle of having sex when Keith came crashing through the bedroom window. He yells, "Mike how could you fuck my girl, you're my fucking brother man! I trusted you with my life." He pulled out a 357 magnum and shot Mike three times. BAM! BAM! BAM! The sound of the gun and my screams were deafening. Then Keith puts the gun inside of his mouth. "I yell, NO!! Please don't." But he didn't listen. He pulled the trigger and blew a hole in his head and his brains splattered all over me.

That was 20 years ago, and today my life is a total mess. I've tried to kill myself three times. The doctors diagnosed me with a mental disorder and committed me to live in a medically supervised low-income housing with other mentally ill patients. I stay sedated most of the time because I'm a danger to myself. I can't forget that awful night when Keith blew off his head. I will never forgive myself for what I did. I wish I'd died the same night as Keith and Mike did. This is a hell from which there is no emancipation. I'm left

FEAR OF THE MIND

here to suffer and be tormented by my mind
forever.

Unsane

I'm Richard, a cocky robber who's seen the good, the bad and the ugly. My friends fondly called me 'Bullet' because they thought I was fast. We were planning to rob a bank and have been doing survelliance for months to plan everything down to the last detail. We're a trio and we've bought masks to wear during this bank op. So I'm wearing the Freddy Krueger mask, the serial killer in 'A Nightmare on Elm Street', there's Carl who's wearing the Jason Voorhees mask from 'Friday, the

FEAR OF THE MIND

Thirteenth' and then there's Ted, who's wearing the Jigsaw killer mask from the 'Saw' franchise.

We meet at the appointed time and sit in my black Jeep Wrangler. Carl's driving while we go over the details once more. Our machine guns were fully loaded, it had a firing capacity of 300 rounds per minute so whoever is behind that counter, better do exactly as we say. Else, someone's going to be deadmeat.

Carl pulls over at the bank's front exit where I and Ted get out and run into the bank, gun pointing up. As planned, Carl parks the car at the exit and joins us a few minutes later. Once inside, I put out a firing shot to get people's attention as is traditional.

"Put your hands up people, this ain't a day to be heroes," I shout.

MARTHA PEREZ

I motion to the clerks looking visibly petrified and throw them big white bags to unload the cash from the bank locker.

"Hurry along now, nice and neat so no one gets killed. Put all the money in the bags and all of you get out alive; one word in protest, you'll be dead before you can blink your eyes," Ted says showing off his gun.

Carl passes around a bag to collect everyone's wallets, watches, and cellphones. A man in his mid forties, tried to send a message to 911 and Carl shot him dead instantly.

"Anyone else fancy dying this way? Anyone?" he shouts. It's pin drop silence and the clerks behind the counter are being closely watched by Ted and me.

"Come on, speed it up" I yell as impatience begins to take hold of me. The sooner we out of here, the better our chances of getting out of here alive with all this cash.

I see a a female customer trying to get up and I promptly beat her down, warning her not to try anything stupid.

2 sacks full, 2 more to go. "Hurry up because you're against a countdown now" I say. Barely two minutes it's our countdown that's begun because I hear cop sirens ringing out.

I, Ted and Carl pull up the two full sacks of cash and head out the back exit but the cops have surrounded the bank building on all four sides. I hear someone speak out over the loudspeaker.

"Put your hands up in the air or else you'll be shot," the voice says. I scan the block, every cop has his gun pointing at us.

There was no way we could fight this.

"Fuck!" I say out loud and drop the bag down. Seeing me give up, Ted also surrenders. But Carl doesn't. He always said he'd fancy his chances being dead than be in prison for life.

"It doesn't have to end this way, put your hands up in the air and drop your gun" the voice speaks again.

"This is your final warning" it says gently.

Carl didn't budge. I look in Carl's direction as the firing shot was released, hitting straight in his chest. I see Carl drop to the ground with blood oozing out of his chest. He dies instantly.

Ted and I were in our early thirties and this was our first major crime; we were rank amateurs who were looking to up our game. Instead we stand here in the courtroom, pleading 'not guilty' to the charges filed against our name. Our public defender dangled the idea of pleading insanity as defense which seemed good to get away from prison. Ted wasn't too enthusiastic about the idea so he chose to go with his 25 year sentence in prison while I was send to a mental institution. I had hoped it'd be respite from prison, but fifteen years was not going to be a cakewalk. When I first walked into the facility, it felt normal. But after just two days, I began to feel the full brunt of this decision. Everyone was crazy here, I clearly didn't belong. I had to pretend to be crazy like them for the remaining fifteen years of my life. First it was just an act, but now it was my daily reality. There's not much interaction here unless it's a group therapy session. The head nurse was a well built woman named Amy Coser who coordinated everything from medicine, to routine check ups, our therapy sessions, and other miscellaneous responsibilities. She wore thick black rimmed glasses and had a resting bitch face. I'd love to piss her off. She's in my cell right now giving instructions.

"We always have group meetings, and give your meds before bedtime." she says.

I'm not remotely interested in her blah blah so look at the corner of the room with a smirk and then begin to walk back and forth as if I couldn't care less.

"Mr.Richard Shepherd, please have a seat and pay attention. I'm not going to wait for you all day" she says firmly.

F*** her big blue eyes, she's talking to me like a child. I'm not a kid and neither am I insane, however only I knew the latter.

FEAR OF THE MIND

"I don't need your stupid medicines" I say exasperated. She has not a clue who she's dealing with.

I see her face redden with anger, her gaze firmly on me. She doesn't bat an eyelid.

I light up my cigarette and let out a puff of smoke and turn to see her reaction.

She turns to nod at the male staff waiting outside; he's of above average built, he comes in and punches my face and pushes me to the floor. My thin body stumbles and falls to the ground. My mouth is bleeding and I try to sit up. No wonder Ted didn't want to come here, I wish he had tried convincing me harder about this being a bad idea.

"You'll have your group therapy session in a bit and he'll ensure you behave," the nurse says, lowering her glass to look at me squarely.

MARTHA PEREZ

The same guy who punched me, grabs my arm and takes me to a group meeting where a few others are already seated. The men beside me are a pair of twins named Luke and Duke, they seem heavily sedated with drugs and have no strength. They're on wheelchairs. This place smells of death and misery, I shouldn't have come here. How am I going to spend the next fifteen years of my life among crazy people and a nurse who should've been part of the WWE pro wrestling team than be a nurse?! My mind is numbing down. How I wish I could drink to drown my sorrow. That's when my eyes see a ray of sunshine seated at the corner, rocking back and forth on a chair, reading a book. She's got long auburn hair that's tied in a loose plait. Her complexion is light yet warm & rosy. She has full pink lips that look like a rosebud. She's got freckles on the bridge of her nose. She could be in her late twenties but I couldn't care about her age. I get up and go to sit next to her, curious by the presence of this beautiful woman in a place like this.

"Hi beautiful" I say enthusiastically.

She continues to read her book, ignoring my greeting so I venture to ask again.

"Hello? What are you reading?"

This time, she looks up at me and eyes me carefully.

'Moby Dick' she answers.

"Well, what's your name? I'm Richard." I say extending my hand to her.

"Tessa," she says as she shakes my hand.

"It's nice meeting you," I say hoping to keep the conversation going, but instead she's lost in her book again. Damn. She's made me look like a fool. But I wasn't going to give up this soon.

"Why are you here Tessa?" I ask. I'm sure that'd catch her attention.

"The same reason you are" she said, not looking up.

Fiesty little thing this one, I mumbled to myself. She gets up, book in hand when a staff calls out my name, "Mr.Shepherd, please sit, the session is about to begin."

What pathetic timing. I turn around to see Tessa walk away. We finish our pathetic, boring session and were sent back to our cells, to sleep. There were no lock here other than simple latches because everyone was sedated enough to be unable to run. However, there were cameras everywhere.

FEAR OF THE MIND

It's an hour after we were sent to sleep that I hear someone crying softly mixed with a few more voices that were yelling and screaming. I open the door of my cell and run in the direction of the sound to find Tessa being physically assaulted by two other crazy women. I try to separate her from the two and take her out. She's frail in my hands so I carry her; I inhale the fragrance of her soft skin and hair. For a moment there, just a fleeting moment, I felt like a knight in shining armour rescuing a damsel in distress. I look upon her gentle face, innocent as a rose and instantly feel affection for her. I take her to my cell and hug her, she was shivering because she was cold. She fell asleep in my arms, holding onto me. After an hour or so, she woke up and looked at me. My heart melts looking at her angelic face.

I could be here all my life if I could see her everyday.

I had to carry her back to her room before we're caught on the security camera. I tiptoe with her back to her cell and decide to meet in the common room next day after breakfast. Tessa began to call me 'Richie' from that day onward and started to follow me around. She was fearful that her cellmates would attack her again and I pacified her that they wouldn't. We read books together and when I could, I would teach some of the crazies card games. I was bored out of my mind and I was thirsting for an adventure. I'm allowed to have visitors and make a call every two months to whoever I wanted. I wanted a trip out with the crazies, get some sex, booze and party the night away. I talked to one of my old friends about arranging it and he readily agreed. We organized the whole shebang as discreetly as we possibly could and we waited patiently for the day to arrive. So the plan was for the five of us, all men and Tessa for who I was personally responsible. She really didn't want to come because she was worried we'd be caught. So the plan is for Friday night where half of the staff takes off for the weekend, less hassle that way. My friend arrives to pick us up as agreed at the back exit. We tip toe from our cells after the lights are shut out but two of them make weird noises and hit their leg on something on the way to the pick up truck. That ruined it as someone from the security hurriedly came to inspect the source of the sound.

"Fuck!" I say in frustration. I'll be getting no sex, no booze, no nothing. I wanted to feel the breeze on my face and get some good time. We go back to the drawing board and agree to try again next Friday evening, and this time, we'll be super careful.

This time everything goes as planned and we're on our way to a party at a local club. The music is loud and everyone's dancing & drinking. Just what I needed. I was eager to get some action in bed so when I saw one of my old girlfriends, a Spanish girl named Valerie while walking down the stairs, I knew I'd wanted to be inside her. I sweet talk into her ears and she agrees. The crazies begin to drink and let themselves loose and wild. I get Tessa some non-alcoholic beverage and tell her to sit on the sofa until we're all back together and leave to head back to the institution. The plan is to get back before 4am. I have an awesome

FEAR OF THE MIND

time with Valerie and my thirst is quenched for now. I go downstairs around 3am to round up the crazies together and check on Tessa. She's nowhere on the sofa. I looked everywhere among all who were dancing and seated at the bar. I head back upstairs to check if she's using any of the rooms. Something was stirring up in my heart, it was a mixture of fear, worry and desperation to find her asap, I knew something was wrong. I go to the first room and find one of the crazies Al having his freak on, he grins from ear to ear on seeing him and I leave him to it. The second room I go to has two girls getting it together; trust me I would've joined them but right now Tessa was all I could of thought of. In my mind, I'm calling out to her 'Tessa where are you?' I see a bunch of men drinking and playing cards in the third room. I ask them if they saw Tessa anywhere around and they said they didn't.

I'm beginning to feel hopeless as I open the fourth room and there she is laying on the bed. I go to wake her up, thinking she may have slept off because she was tired.

"Tessa, wake up sweetie, we got to get going," I say touching her hands. I freeze. Her hands are cold.

"Tessa!" I say as I get closer to hear her heartbeat, I hear nothing. She wasn't breathing. I give her CPR in the hope her heart would start beating again. Nothing. Not a beat. I was too late! She's gone. My tears begin to fall on her face as I'm unable to fathom what happened when my foot hits a man lying on the floor with his pants down.

FEAR OF THE MIND

My brain just bursts into unrestrained rage. I choke him to death with every ounce of energy in me. I didn't care about what came next. This jerk raped her and killed her, he went a little too far to satisfy himself. This was all my fault, I should've let her be. She never wanted to come, I was the one who forced her to come and have

fun with us. And now she's not coming back.

I was charged for murder and was given the death penalty. I welcomed my sentence because I couldn't bear the guilt of Tessa's death on me for the rest of my living life, dying was a far better proposition. The day of my execution arrives; a priest prays with me. I'm taken to the gas chamber and strapped to the chair. All I can see in my mind is Tessa's face, her innocence radiating like heavenly light. I didn't feel an iota of guilt for killing the guy who ended her life. He didn't deserve to live and neither did I. It was fair game. I close my eyes and say my peace, waiting for God to set me free.

Then I started singing an old Negro Spiritual song that my Momma used to sing while cooking me some Hamhocks, Collard greenes, and Cornbread–"Free at Last, Thank God, I'm Free at Last!" Lord Have Mercy on my   Soul.

Trust

My car is broke and I don't have any money to get it fixed, so I'm walking home instead of catching the bus. My feet are hurting from wearing cheap shoes that I bought at Dollar General. I work there and receive a 25% employee discount off all merchandise. How could I resist, right? Anyway, as I walk home, I come to the corner of Trust Street & Malcolm Blvd. It's about 6.30 pm and it usually takes me about 40 minutes to walk home, which means I'd be home approximately by 7.30 pm. However, there's a short cut if I go left down 'Trust Street' which would cut the time by half, so I could be home in 20 minutes flat. I decide to take the short route and turn left on 'Trust Street'. I'm always skeptical when someone says, "Trust me" because I always read it as a red flag that warns me of "someone wanting to trick or deceive me. Why would anyone name a road 'Trust Street' anyway?" It's almost pitch dark except for a few lights coming from the homes closeby and from the headlights of cars that are passing by. So I brave up and decide to walk down the dark and lonely road even though my feet feel like they're dragging rocks.

I keep walking until I come to the part of the road where there are no houses; it's lonely and feels creepy. I stop to look behind me and get an eerie feeling that someone is following so I pick up my pace. Suddenly I feel a pair of hands cover my face and mouth; unable to scream and stricken with fear, I lose conciousness. When I wake up, I'm in a dark room with no windows. It's just cemented walls and floor with a single bed; my hands are handcuffed to the bedpost. I look down at my body shocked. "Oh MY GOD!" I gasp. I'm nude and my head hurts really bad, like someone hit me with the sole intention of knocking me out and to bring me here.

I hear the sound of keys dangling. OMG! I panic not knowing what lays ahead. The door finally opens and a tall muscular man walks in. His green eyes betray no emotion. His dirty blonde hair is slicked back into a pony tail. He's worn a plain black t-shirt and jeans. He walks over to me and puts his hand over my mouth. My eyes feel like they are going to pop out of my head and my body trembles with fear. He lets go and then takes the handcuffs off and says, "Sit up, Peggy Barnett," My eyes widen in surprise, he knew my name!

"My name is Sean Lawrence. I'm going to tell you the rules of living here in my home. First, I chose you to be my slave, and you will obey me. I've been following you for months– you're beautiful in the nude I might add. I won't hurt you if you do everything I say. Do you trust what I'm telling you?"

I nod, "Yes, I trust you."

What else could I say? Hell, no I don't trust you? For a split second, I thought about the road I shouldn't have taken 'Trust Street'. The irony of it all.

He smiles, "Good girl I'm going to fuck you until I get tired."

I'm scared and my voice starts to crackle. "So you're going to rape me?" I say.

"Well, yes I am. But you'll grow to like it in time."

I can't believe this is happening to me.

He said, "Have you had sex before?"

I uttered, "uh huh."

"What did you say?"

"Yes, I have."

"Okay, good."

He takes me to another bed in an adjacent room with simalarly cemented walls and no windows. He lays me on navy blue silk sheets and starts to kiss me and pulls my hair to look at him. He says, "Your blue eyes are divine, your skin is soft and you have some luscious

lips."

His husky voice muttering these compliments would've had a totally different and opposite effect had it been under normal circumstances. So it was of no surprise that it had no effect on me.

I turn my head sideways so he wouldn't kiss me.

"Do you want me to hit you?" he asks, his tone of voice now laced with frustration and anger.

"No, please don't hurt me." I say.

FEAR OF THE MIND

"Then stop resisting. My mouth is watering to taste your lovely gifts." He says, his voice relaxing again.

He puts nipple clamps on each one of my nipples. It was so painful that I wanted to holler, but then five minutes later the pain subsided and to my surprise, it felt good. He puts his finger inside my vagina and sucks on his finger. "Hmmm! You're fine, baby and taste like juicy fruit. Do you see what you do to me?"

I said, "Yes." He takes the handcuffs off and cuffs each wrist on the bedposts instead. He licks and sucks on my nipples. I had read someplace that if you are being raped, don't resist and pretend that you enjoy it. So I decided to try and enjoy it. At first, I felt ashamed because what he was doing to me felt good. He put his two fingers in my vagina and then made me suck his fingers. I start crying, "No please."

He said, "Stop crying I'm not going to hurt you! You are my treasure and I'm going treat you like a good slave. One day, you will beg me to fuck you. I'm very kind and rich and now that I own you, don't try to escape because then

I will most certainly hurt you."

He touches my clitoris, and starts licking it and pushes his fingers deep inside me. He tells me to suck his fingers again, it tastes sweet and salty then he puts his erection into my pussy. I started to squirm and move my body in response.

He covers my mouth wickedly and thrust his cock inside me harder and harder. I began to moan loudly when suddenly covers my mouth with his and kisses me deeply. I grab his shirt, holding it tight and I climax so strong like I've never done before.

He rolls off of me and turns me on top of him, he says, "I told you, you would like it."

All I could do is nod in agreement. But inside my mind and the reality was that he fucking raped me.

Sean takes off the handcuffs and puts on a blindfold and takes me to the shower.

He lathers my body with soap and drapes me with a soft towel. Then takes me back to the cold room of horrors. He takes the towel with him and leaves me standing there naked. I will surely catch pneumonia if I stay here. I remove the blindfold and see a white robe and that the bed is made up with clean sheets. There sitting on the night stand is a cup of hot coffee and a full meal consisting of a small steak with fresh steamed veggies and salad. I eat it like a starving alley cat while staring at my surroundings. What will I do if he leaves me here? I need to do something. He wants me to be his slave, so I needed to win his trust if I'm going to escape. I needed to be his sweet belle until I can find a way out of this hell.

Weeks had gone by, and one night he invited me to his house upstairs. The stone cold cemented room was an isolated part of his basement. I'm guessing if he's invited me to dinner in his house I may have won his trust after all. I played the coy, humble slave all this time in the hope somewhere, someday I'd have an opportunity to escape. I head upstairs for dinner wondering if that long awaited

FEAR OF THE MIND

opportunity is tonight. He had made dinner and set it across the elegant dining room table. I look around, taking in this new environment, a welcome change from the closed dark walls of the basement. We sit down for dinner and he told me stories about him being abused as a kid; it was immensely personal and really detailed. His confiding in me was a sure sign of him trusting me.

After dinner, I ask him, "Would you like me

to wash the dishes?"

He was on the phone, he nods his head and whispers, "Yes, yes."

I head for the kitchen looking for a door in the living room area but it had several locks on it. Then I go to the kitchen reluctantly and start looking for a knife but there were only but a few spoons and forks.

I remembered what I was taught in a self defense class earlier, that anything can be used as a weapon. I looked at the fork thinking how I could use it and decide to put it in my pocket. Just then, he walked into the kitchen and stared at me with suspicion.

"Peggy, what are you doing with that fork?" he asks, mildly irritated.

I said, "I'm putting it in the dishwasher."

He said, "Stop, you're lying. I warned you not to get on my bad side."

He grabs me by my hair and takes the fork and sticks me on my arm then drags me like ragdoll. He throws me into the cemented room and locks the door behind me. Thirty minutes later, he comes back in there and slaps my face repeatedly. He says, "I'm going to spank you, you've been a bad girl."

He puts me over his lap stomach down. He pulls my panties down and with a firm hand, slaps my ass until my ass was sore and stinging with pain. It was the worse beating I'd ever had. Then he threw me on the bed and fucked me hard. Afterward, he said he had no further use for me. And he was thinking about killing me like he did the other girls he brought as slaves or let me go if I didn't tell on him.

I said, "Yes, I promise. I won't tell anyone."

He said, "I will let you go in seven days if you do everything I ask you to do."

I agreed, and over the next week we engaged in various forms of S&M bondage, and he fucked me in my ass every day. He seemed to like that more than anything–what a fucking lunatic.

Seven days later, he was true to his word. I stood there like a child while he dressed me in a black dress, a white blouse, and high heels. Then he blindfolded me and drove me to the same street where he kidnapped me from.

"Get out the car Peggy and don't you try and look at my tags or I will come back for you." He warned.

I said, "Thank you. I won't tell anybody."

I walked home, but something was missing.

I wasn't the same person anymore. I didn't even

think about calling the cops. I began craving for sex, something I hadn't felt in the past.

FEAR OF THE MIND

One night, several weeks later, I went to a nightclub. I was wearing a short leather skirt, a tight blouse and knee-high leather boots. I was on the floor dancing by myself and this guy came up behind me and started dancing with me. We talked a bit and had a few drinks. "Then he said "Let's get out of here and go to my place."

When we got to his place, he put on some soft music and poured me a glass of wine. After some small talk, he said, "Let's play a card game and whoever loses would have to be a slave and be submissive to the winner."

I said, "I don't know if I want to play that game."

He said, "Trust me, it will be fun."

I said, "Trust me? Is that what you said?"

"Yes, you can trust me.," he said.

185

I look at him, trying to gauge him. Can't trust a man who says "Trust me" ever.

I reluctantly agree.

"Okay, let's play."

After a few rounds of the card game, I emerged as the winner.

He said, "I'm your humble slave."

I said, "I want to tie you to the bed.

"Okay darling, anything you want?"

It was happening all over again. I couldn't stop it. I felt evil running through my veins. I fucked this guy's brains out and made him eat my pussy. When I finished with him, I became a raving maniac and cut his dick off. I stuck it in his mouth and left him tied to the bedposts.

Since then I've had many one-night stands and brutally killed three men. Each one said, "Trust Me."

FEAR OF THE MIND

Whenever I hear those two words, it brings back memories of walking home, down that dark road called 'Trust Street'. It makes me furious and lose all control self-control.

Never trust anyone that says "Trust Me." Let it be a WARNING. It's the cryout out of the guilty– all they want to do is fool you, rip you off, or like in my case fuck you.

Someday I hope to find the guy who raped me. I know he'd be proud of the monster that I've become–but this time things would be different.

Winning Ticket

I work as a manager at the Ace market. I've been through an ugly divorce; the woman who was once the center of my world had cheated on me with my best friend. The two people I held most dear to my heart wedged the most painful betrayal to my heart. She took away everything I had ever worked for and left me with little consolation – my car, a few clothes and paltry few dollars to ensure that I'd survive as a newly divorced single man. I was heartbroken and lonely, I worked hard at my

FEAR OF THE MIND

job and keeping busy kept me distracted from playing the negative self-pity loop in my head.

It's a bright and sunny Monday morning and we have a new woman start work today. Her name is Nelly McGraw. At 5ft 2', she's a petite but attractive woman with the face of a doll. She had shoulder length blonde hair and a surprisingly raucous voice, which she used to her advantage. She came across as a hard working person with a strong sense of ethics during her interview. She was nonchalant and street smart, something that's of immense value in a crowded, competitive work environment. I had looked forward to her joining the team because after the divorce, she's probably the first woman I've been physically and mentally attracted to. Not that she knows and I don't intend to play around with her. Technically speaking, I'm her boss and if I've to keep my workforce in check, I need to keep myself in check.

I keep an eye on her as the store opens for business; she's yelling around like she owns the place, an off putting but necessary quality if you have to survive here. Meaning, she was being a total bitch and she couldn't care less. Aside from work, I didn't have too many hobbies or rather I didn't indulge in much with one exception–lottery tickets. I had lost so much in the divorce that buying lottery tickets had become a daily obsession. I played the same numbers day after day, thinking to myself that one day I'll win and make up for all this loss in life. I'm suddenly woken from my reverie with Nelly's voice ringing in my ears loud and clear.

FEAR OF THE MIND

"You daydreaming? There's work around here that needs to be done. You mind helping me lift this box?" she says, eyeing me head to toe.

I feel like she's the one talking like the manager now. I roll my eyes but don't move to help, curious to know how she'll react.

"You men are full of shit." She says as she bends down to lift the heavy box.

"Who's the manager, you or me?" I ask, knowing that this would provoke her.

She straightens up and gives me a stare; if looks could kill, that stare would be it.

"Fiesty baby," I respond with a chuckle.

"I'm not your baby" she says shaking her head.

I like the way this litte exchange is going.

"You're not even my type," she says with a straight face.

"Why? Because I'm black?" I ask, trying to sound as non-intrusive as possible.

"That has nothing to do with it, so stop talking to me and start working Mr.Manager" she quips sarcastically.

I laughed so hard hearing her response that my face turned red. Something about this exchange with her breathed new life into me, I never felt so alive. It's like I'd received an electric jolt to bring me back to life. I looked at Nelly as she continued on with her work; I didn't know what was the future of this connection but I knew she'd already made an impression on me.

FEAR OF THE MIND

The week went by quickly, Nelly had settled into her new work routine and the other staff were picking up on her vivacious energy. She had dropped it casually that she was married. When I heard it, I thought maybe I was never going to get lucky, like ever. I was just beginning to think may be, just maybe, there was a chance this would become something. To say I was disappointed would be an understatement.

It was Friday, and as is routine, I and some staff would head to Applebee's for dinner and some drinks. I had planned on asking Nelly to join us when she came in this morning. She was a stickler for time and never came late so it wasn't a surprise seeing her stride in at sharp 8.45am. But what I didn't expect was my dick to twitch on seeing her today. She had worn red lipstick making her lusciously beautiful mouth even more lascivious. Her flawless skin was glowing and rosy; her hair was tied off in a messy bun like she had just woken up like this. I couldn't take my eyes off her. My heart skipped a beat as she walked closer to where I stood. I wish I could indulge in some day time fantasy because this woman turns me on like nothing else can but there's mundane work by the dozen to be finished before I can even think of anything else. Besides, when I look at her, I keep forgetting that she's married!

Just seeing her energy makes me work harder. She throws herself into her work with a passion that's hard to match and it's had a positive effect on everyone.

FEAR OF THE MIND

We're about to break for lunch so I walk up to her to dangle the idea of hanging out after work for a few drinks.

"Nelly, it's a kinda work tradition here to catch up for dinner and drinks at Applebee's on

weekends. Would you like to join us?"

I see her eyes hesitate.

"It's only dinner with coworkers, nothing to get worked up about" I say reassuringly.

"Okay Mr.Manager" she says nodding her head with a smile.

I'm pretty sure I look like a fool right now with a ear-to-ear grin plastered on my face.

"One day, you'll beg me for a kiss" I say. I love to get a reaction out of her.

"I'd rather die than give you a kiss you aren't worthy of." she says flashing a seductive smile.

"So I gather your husband is worthy then?" I say with sarcasm in my voice.

"Shut up," she says laughingly and gives me a look that says there's something more here than meets the eye.

I can't wait to get this day over with and head out for dinner.

It's 7pm and we all meet up at the restaurant. We order drinks and appetizers to get the evening going. I can see Nelly having fun and letting herself loose as the evening unwinds. She's smoking HOT! I could see through her silky navy blue blouse that she wasn't wearing a bra. She had decent sized breasts, just the way I liked them. She had worn a pair of tight jeans and a pair of strappy black heels. She looked like a modern day Marilyn Monroe.

She probably won't fancy a black man, a low profile manager that has dreams of winning the lotto someday. I'm an easy going guy with simple needs, my only indulgence being lottery tickets. Nelly was a gorgeous woman and I knew she'd probably never leave her husband for me.

Nelly sits next to me drinking her glass of wine; she has an infectious laugh that puts everyone at ease. The evening was filled with jokes and innuendos, the drinks kept coming. Nelly was holding up alright but was visibly drunk.

"Trevon, could you take me to your house tonight? I can't go home drunk, Lester would get angry if he knew I was drinking." Nelly asks me as she bats her eyelids innocently.

"Okay, I got you covered" I say and escort her to my car. She makes a call to her husband to say she's going to spend the night with one of her girlfriends and will be home tomorrow by brunch.

I drive home quietly, wondering what's the

night ahead going to be like.

We reach home and I show her the guest bedroom in my small condo. My mind is filled with nasty thoughts, I tried resisting but couldn't. I've not been with a woman in a long time and with Nelly, somehow, everything felt very natural, like she belonged here in this moment, in this room. It's when I'm thinking all this that I hear Nelly's voice.

FEAR OF THE MIND

"Trey?" she says.

"Yes?, I'm right here" I say looking into her deep set eyes.

"Could you hold me?" she asks, almost puppy faced.

I take off my shirt and wrap my arms around her petite frame. I feel the sweet vanilla scent off her neck. She turns around to gaze at me.

She brings her face closer to mine and our lips touch, our tongues fighting inside each other's mouth as we surrender to the passion that's consuming us. Our hands caress, touch, and swirl over each other's bodies in an irresistable frenzy of emotion. We made love all night like we'd never before.

The next morning, things felt remarkably different. We made love once more before she left for her house. We both knew we'd fallen in love but she refused to accept it for a few weeks, feeling guilty about cheating on her husband. Eventually however, she decided to leave him for me. For once, I felt like the luckiest man in the world. This beautiful woman was mine and I made sure she knew how much she meant to me each day. We worked hard to make a fresh start. We were like a honeymooning couple, unable to contain our passion for each other whether it was at work or at home. We made love everywhere, in the bathroom, at the storeroom, in the car, we just couldn't keep our hands off each other. She finally filed for divorce and moved in with me. Once the shiny exterior of our new love had faded, we got a reality check. Nelly hated that I spent money on buying lotto tickets everyday; I had to sell off the condo to make ends meet.

Nelly would often scream in frustration "Trey, you need to get an extra job, else we'd be broke and on the streets before we know it!"

Years passed and our love was beginning to cool. Good thing we didn't have any kids in the midst of this, else things would've been a whole lot more difficult. We didn't share much in common anymore but I never stopped loving her. I lost my job and eventually she lost hers too. We were in a tight spot financially and had only each other to lean on. We'd go days without talking, I don't remember when was the last time I kissed her or she kissed me with the kind of passion we first had. We were a big mess. I was afraid that I'd lose her. However, despite how grim things seemed to be, I never lost faith that I would win the lotto with those numbers I played with every day. I'll be a rich man one day and I'll buy, my baby, a brand new house, a car and that trip to Europe we'd always dreamed of. We also wanted a dog. I know things will be different someday, I believe it!

As always, I hear Nelly's voice cut through my thoughts. "Trey!! Did you find a job?"

"No!" I shout in anger.

" Did you buy the milk I told you to buy?" she asks in a disgruntled voice.

"No," I say again, not wanting to start a fight.

"What about my cigarettes?" she continues.

"Sorry Nelly, I didn't buy any of that. All I bought were my lottery tickets" I said.

FEAR OF THE MIND

"You're a worthless man Trey, a dreamer who has nothing to offer." She said indignantly. She continued as if to provoke me into saying something.

"Lester at least had a job and a home you know? Going home with you that night was just my bad luck!" she said, her pretty face twisted in irritation.

"Don't throw stones at me about your ex Nelly. That's a low blow bring him in our fights." I say, trying to keep my temper under check.

"Shut the fuck up Trey, we are sinking underwater! There's no money and no job." She shouted and stormed out of the room. We kept fighting like this almost everyday. We received unemployment benefits from which we made ends meet; we lived miserably. We loved each other and were reluctant to leave each other no matter how dire the situation seemed. Two months later, I found a job that paid off the bills and kept us afloat. It was tough and Nelly reminded me to live in the real world and not keep day dreaming like I usually do. Nelly worked two jobs and I felt bad that I couldn't provide her the life she had always dreamed of.

One day morning, I woke up with a strong, unshakeable feeling that I should get the mortgage money and go to Vegas to try my hand at the jackpot. When I told Nelly, she said it was a bad idea but I was insistent so she reluctantly agreed. We rented a car and left for Vegas on the same day. I lost all the money in the Vegas and we returned empty. I had to sell off my guitar, the one that my Dad gave to me on his deathbed for a mere hundred dollars just to buy some gas and food for the return trip home. I was devastated that my hunch had been so wrong. Nelly didn't speak to me for a month after we returned from that trip.

Things got worse from there on between her and me. I couldn't blame her. She kept saying things that made me lose whatever little confidence I had left. She called me a 'unlucky dreamer', that I kept making mistakes and that I could get nothing right.

However, I still kept buying my lottery tickets, I hadn't lost faith in that.

Seasons changed, years passed. I was eighty years old, living in a convalescent home. Nelly was seventy years old and lived in a separate room adjacent to mine. She was so miffed and bitter that she didn't even want to be in the same room as me. We visit each other once in awhile to read a book or watch something on television. I never stopped buying the lottery ticket. It had become an odd routine for me, an undying habit that had stuck with me through thick and thin.

One day, I walk to seven eleven to buy Nelly a coffee and my lottery ticket. That night, I settled into my chair to watch the winning number. I could recognize that number anywhere in the world because I'd been playing those same numbers for decades. The winning number was 758904! I had won the lotto! I was in complete shock! I couldn't move my legs as they were stiff from my arthritis but I wanted to jump up and down. Instead I took little tiny steps to tell Nelly that we were finally rich! That she'd have that house she always dreamed of, and a brand new car and maybe even a five star holiday.

"Nelly, Nelly" I say with a trembling voice.

"What? I'm watching a good movie, don't disturb me" she says as she continues to keep her eyes on the television.

"Baby I won!" I say excitedly.

She turned sideways to look at me. "Won what?"

"The lotto" I said waving the winning ticket in my hands.

"Give me that fucking ticket Trey. you You owe me a lot." Nelly said putting her hands out

motioning me to hand over the ticket to her.

All my excitement went out the window. I thought Nelly would share in this happiness, instead she was only thinking about herself.

"I signed it already. You are a selfish bitch with no brains. I told you that someday I'll win." I said angrily.

"Get the fuck out of my room! Get out!!" she screamed angrily.

I walked out of the room with trembling hands and legs, my voice quivering with emotion. I went to my room with tears in my eyes. I lay in bed clutching my ticket tightly, thinking about this Pyrrhic victory. I had loved Nelly through thick and thin and it broke my heart that it all unraveled in such a heartbreaking manner. I looked at my favorite chocolate pudding that was resting on my table, a dessert I always looked forward to. But today, I had no appetite for it. That night, I heard commotion in Nelly's room, nurses running in and out, the sound of monitors and buzzers going off. I wanted to rush to her room to see what was happening but was unable to get up. I lay awake, anxiously waiting for someone to tell me what had caused such a stir in the middle of the night. A few minutes later, a nurse walked in and informed that Nelly had died of a heart attack.

I'm devastated at the news, the irony of this day gnawed at my heart. I had won the lotto the same day as my wife died. And more than anything else, Nelly had passed away still angry at me. We couldn't share even a moment of happiness at the stroke of good fortune and all of it was utterly meaningless. I sobbed that night, not wanting to live another day. I held on to the ticket and drifted off to sleep.

MARTHA PEREZ

"Wake up Trevon, time to have breakfast. Oh My   God Trevon! Code blue, Code blue." The nurse shouts over the buzzer.

Trevon passed away the same night as Nelly, only a few hours later. The winning ticket had fallen to the floor and was swept away by the cleaning staff to the trash. No one won. What a life.

Gentlemen's Club

My mom is a single parent, who works as a housekeeper, she doesn't make much money. She is a gorgeous woman and I look like her. But I don't want to be a house-keeper. It is embarrassing when kids ask me what my mom does for a living. I just can't help thinking if things were different. I just turned sixteen, and I want to buy things and go places. I've always wanted to be a dancer. Ever since my friend Ella told me that her older sister dancing for a nightclub, the idea has been swirling around in my head. She said they're looking for young girls aged 18 to 21 years with a beautiful body.

So today I'm going to apply for a job at the Gentlemen's Club, and it would be my first job. I'll have to keep it quiet and tell Mom that I'm working at a fast food restaurant or something. She really doesn't check on me much. I'm pretty much left to do my own thing. My mom has a no-good boyfriend that comes over a lot. His name is Tim; he cheats on her & screams at her almost all the time. I don't know why she puts up with him. The last time they got into a big argument, he was yelling, pointing his finger in her face and called her a bitch. I'm protective of Mom; I don't like anyone treating her mean like Tim did. I got a knife and cut him on his arm. However, Mom called the cops on me. Can you believe it? The cops put me in handcuffs, all because I was trying to defend my mother. She told them that I hadn't taken my medication in a week and I was out of control. I do admit that I have a terrible temper and when I get upset, I can't control my anger. Tim didn't press charges or I'd have been sent to jail or Juvenile Detention. Well, anyway, my mother deserves better. My father died when I was eight years old in a car accident, and I've never gotten over it. He was the best Dad in the world. I don't plan on going to college, but I don't want to be a damn housekeeper either. I want the finer things in life; money, fancy cars, beautiful clothes, and someone to love me right.

"Hey Mom, I'm going to look for a job, see you later!"

"Okay, Honey. Try McDonald's they always hire teenagers."

"Yea, okay Mom."

"Don't be late for dinner, Wendy." I hear her say on my way out the door.

I have to catch two buses to get downtown to the Gentleman's Club. I'm wearing skinny jeans, a black sweater, and some sexy high heels. I have left my long brown hair open today so it covers my waist.

When I arrive, I'm in awe. The place is elegant with chandeliers hanging from the ceilings, blue velvet seats and cherry wood tables. It's an awesome place. The stage has ten poles where the girls dance.

FEAR OF THE MIND

A man greets me, "Hello beautiful, how can

I help you?" He's kind of flirty, who greets

someone like that. I was a bit nervous.

"I would like to apply for a job?" I ask my voice quivering with excitement.

"Well, I'm the manager; all of our waitress positions are filled."

"No sir, I want to work as a dancer."

"Oh, I see." He looks me up and down like I'm a China Doll or something. He extends his hand to shake, saying "Okay, my name is Dan Cooper.

"My name is Wendy Wagner, glad to meet you." I respond shaking his hand firmly. Not bad, huh? I'm very confident talking to adults.

I'm not the shy type. I always act older than my age.

"Okay, right this way, please."   I follow him to his office. He's tall & handsome with golden brown hair and hazel eyes. He was lean but muscular.

"Have a seat, what is your name again, baby doll?"

"Wendy Wagner" I say, rolling my eyes. He's eyeing me in a way that's making me uncomfortable.

"Look here, let's get one thing straight. I didn't come here to fuck you; I came here to see if I can get a job as a dancer." I say assertively and assuredly.

"Whoa! hold on here. You are a feisty one, aren't you?" he says with a smile dancing on his lips.

FEAR OF THE MIND

"Sorry, I like to lay my cards on the table, right up front so you know where I'm coming from."

"Okay. I understand. What can I do for you?"

"I want to apply for a job as a stripper."

"Really. You're too young."

"I heard girls my age, are working here, I'm 18 and soon to be 19." I had already planned to lie about my age, but what the heck, I want this job.

"They work in the back because it's against the law to have you out front. This is a gentleman's club and men would be putting their hands all over you." He said, as if I couldn't handle it.

"Hey, I know what it is." I say in a matter fact kinda voice.

"Can you dance?"

"Well yes... no, but I can learn. I'm a fast learner. I'll be your top dancer and make more money for you than any of your other girls." I could see that he felt my confidence by the look

on his face.

"Really. Are you shy or coy by any chance? Because that is certainly not something we want in this job." he says.

I say, "Of course not."

"Well, stand up and take your clothes off." He says in a commanding way.

I didn't complain. I take off my sweater and slowly take off my jeans. Dan stares at my every move. I'm standing in my bra and pant-ies.

FEAR OF THE MIND

He twitches his mouth and clears his throat and says, "Please, remove your bra and panties." He looks more nervous asking me to do this than me stripping down nude.

I do as he requests. I'm standing nude right in front of him. I try to cover my private parts. This is the first time I've ever displayed my whole body in naked in front of someone; I bet even my doctor hasn't seen me this naked since my birth.

Dan says, "Don't cover yourself, Wendy; there will be hundreds of guys coming to see that unbelievable body of yours."

I slowly remove my hands. I feel self-conscious in a way that I haven't felt before.

"Wow, you have a beautiful body. You're right; you could one day be the top dancer here someday and rake in all the money."

"Thanks." I mutter.

"Okay, the first thing you have to do is get waxed."

"What's that?" I say.

"Shave your pubic hair. You have a bush down there. Most men won't like it and it's not good hygiene."

"What?!!" I ask in surprise. I've never heard

that before. My mom told me never cut it. "Okay, I'll do it. Does that mean I have the job?"

"Yes. I'm going to give you $500 advance so you can buy some sexy lingerie, lacy satin costumes, racy mesh teddies, some corsets, garter belts. The less you wear, the better. My assistant Valentina will go with you and help you shop. The more you tease, the more you please and the more money you'll make. You'll have to take some dance classes here and study the dances of the other girls for two weeks."

"Thank you, Dan," I say pleased hearing the proposition and get dressed quickly.

"Don't thank me; just remember you have a lot to learn about this business."

"No problem. I want to learn everything." I say enthusiastically.

"Well, sometimes I may want to have sex with you. I will gladly pay $1,000 each time for your services.

I give him a disgusting look and he said, "Oh I'm just joking," and starts laughing.

"Yea, right." I didn't know whether he was joking or not so I just played it off, although for a brief second $1,000 did sound appealing.

MARTHA PEREZ

It's been about 15 days and today is my last day of dance classes. It has been exhausting, you really have to be in shape as a dancer. Each show is about an hour long. I have blisters on my hands and feet from holding and sliding down the poles. I couldn't even walk for a couple of days–fuck this has been harder than I thought.

I'm glad the day is over. When I get home, mom left me a note. It reads, "Sorry honey I didn't
have time to cook dinner, I had to help a friend with a situation." You're on your own tonight."

I could use some 'me' time. So I cooked myself a chilidog and for dessert, I had only one Twinkie. I'd have gladly had another one like I usually do, but I didn't want to look fat.

Finally the day I've been prparing for is here. It's showtime and I'm ready. I met the girls backstage who'll be dancing with me tonight on stage. They are all beautiful and much older than me. Christina is a tall blonde, Lee is short with red hair and a cute body. Carmen has bleach blonde hair, tall with lots of curves, Debbie has long ash brown hair, cut in layers; she's petitie and way too thin if you ask me. Liz has shoulder length hair & nice body and so does Connie who has long brown hair. With the exception of Debbie, we're all voluptuous, well-endowed young women. I overheard some of the girls laughing and talking about me saying that I'm going to fall on my ass tonight, but I'm not going to let that bother me. I know what I'm capable of. I will have all the guys wanting and begging for me. I saw a quote written on the windshield of an old broken down car on my way to work today, "Do not dream your life, live your dream." And that's what I intend on doing starting tonight.

I'm wearing a short, pleated black skirt, a white blouse tied up, fishnets stockings and spike heels. I have makeup on, lipstick, and my long brown hair has been cut in layers to cover my shoulders.

I saw the movie "Striptease" this weekend and learned a lot from watching Demi Moore.

Al, is the manager for the striptease club. He's probably as experienced as Dan in managing the girls. He says, "You're next baby,"

FEAR OF THE MIND

I give him, a smile. I had picked the song 'Baby Hit Me One More Time' by Britney Spears. I'm breathing fast, but I'm also feeling confident that I'll arouse the crowd.

I hear Al onstage, announce, "Okay gentleman, I want you to put your hands together and welcome to the stage the sexy and sultry dancer, Preciosa."

Preciosa was the stage name picked for me, which was just a twist on 'Precious'. I walk to the stage with a sassy walk and an innocent look on my face. I have to learn how to play the crowd. Dan told me that men are fascinated by young women that are innocent looking. The men are yelling my name 'Preciosa', and saying,

"Take your clothes off baby!"

MARTHA PEREZ

I feel like a princess adorned in pearls. I start to dance to the beat. My hands are moving up and down my body.

"Hey take your top off," a man yells.

Not yet, I say to myself. I need to work the crowd a bit more. I squat to the floor and come back up. I hear more screams, "Work it, baby." I twist my hips and roll my stomach like an island girl. I pull my head back holding the pole and wrap my right leg around it. I'm dancing with the pole like it's part of me. Then I slowly remove my blouse and my shorts, showing a black shelf bra and G-string. The men are going crazy. They're holding heaps of dollar bills in their hands. I snap my bra off shaking my tits and slowly remove my G-string, showing off my freshly shaved pussy. Everyone screams, "Yeah!!! Yeah!!!!" I started to sway my hips with my hand touching my tits. The crowd is yelling for more, so I start shaking my ass more vigorously. I then lay on the floor, raising my hips up in the air to the beat of the music and when it got to the chorus line "Hit me with your love" I acted as if I had reached a climax.

I hear Al's voice say, "Gentlemen, that's Preciosa! Isn't she great!? Let's give her a big hand." The men stood up, yelling my name "Preciosa." I put my bra and panties back on. The men began to stick heaps of money into my stockings; ten and twenty dollar bills and even some $100 bills. I mingle in the crowd for 30 minutes and money is flying every-where.

Dan hollers, "Hey, no touching her."

I go backstage to count all my money. I

made two thousand dollars with a single dance.

I was ecstatic. Just then a security guard appears asking me to meet the boss at his office. Yesss! I guess he wants to congratulate me. When I get there, Dan is on the phone. He points to the chair and whispers, "Sit down." When he finishes the call, he grins like a cat that ate the canary and says, "Wendy, darling, you were fabulous tonight. Let's celebrate." He pops open a bottle of champagne, a 1969 Vintage. "For you, nothing but the best." I didn't know whether it was the best or not because it's the first time I've ever had alcohol.

He raises his glass and taps mine, "Here's a toast to us."

The wine tasted real sweet and I drank it like soda pop. I was really thirsty from dancing. I drank it a little too fast and it went straight to my head. Then I asked for more. He was smiling at me and says, "I want you to practice how to give a private dance and I want you to practice it on me."

I said, "Okay!" The other girls told me how much money they were making giving clients PD's so sure, why not? I was feeling good and I did need the practice. So I take off my clothes and sit on his desk with my G-String on. I open my legs. I move the G-String around on my pussy, pulling it up and down. I was getting wet. Dan moves the G-String to the side to take a peek. "Oh baby I like your muffin, spread your legs so I can explore your sweetness." Then he tears my panties with his teeth. He kisses my inner lips and circles my clitoris with his tongue. Then he licks it and holds it between his teeth, sucking it–driving me insane. He starts fucking my vagina with his tongue, and I start to move and holler "More Oh! Yes, Dan! More! I'm cumming." He's licking my pussy relentlessly. Then he inserts his big cock in my tight pussy from behind and bangs me roughly. I have another orgasm. He kisses my ass, turns me around and says, "You're mine now, I own you. You don't fuck any other guy unless they pay you two thousand dollars, if you do, you will pay the consequences. I'm the master of your universe now and I will protect you and take care of you."

I roll my eyes and put my clothes on. I say, "I'm nobody's slave. It was just a fuck, you idiot." I leave his office and slam the door.

FEAR OF THE MIND

I take a secret exit out of building meant for the dancers and take a taxi home instead of the bus. I made so much money and wanted to treat myself, so no more public transportation for me. I kept 10% of my earnings and gave the rest to Dan. That's our arrangement. It didn't seem fair but he explained that he had over-head to pay.

When I get home, it's well past 3am and my mom is fast asleep. Thank goodness, I didn't need to hear her mouth tonight. I want to take a hot shower and wash the night away. I thought, so this is what it's like to be famous? I can get used to it. I want to be the best dancer so I had to add new dance routines every time I perform. So I start searching the internet. I'm going to save all my money and invest it in a business of some kind. I'm only 16 so I can learn a lot.

Tonight is the Gentleman's Club 20th anniversary party. The biggest show of the year. I notice a good-looking guy, I've seen him somewhere before. He wears black glasses inside the club as if to conceal his identity. His face screams money and he always sat in the VIP section all alone. I've never seen him smile. Well, tonight I'm going to cater to him and make him want me. I'm going to smile and shake my ass especially for him.

The club is packed and all the girls are perked up, full of energy and doing a great job. All of them are dancing their asses off and getting paid. Al's voice has become familiar to me, so when he begins announcing, I know it's my turn.

FEAR OF THE MIND

"Here's who you've been waiting for all night, the beautiful   Preciosa!" I come out wearing a cowboy hat some boots, and a see through lace coral dress, swaying to the beat of the   music.   I   walk   on   stage   swaying provocatively and had all the guys eating out of my hands. I was tracing my body with my hands. I took my dress off while shaking my ass. The men whistled and screamed to take all my clothes off. I'm touching my tits and my nipples had become hard. I threw my bra out to the handsome guy sitting all alone. I did my new dance routine and all the men went crazy. The men were pulling at me while I was dancing and throwing $20 and $50 bills on the stage; there was so much money on the stage that I didn't know how to collect it all. There were security guards all around the stage to protect me and the money. It was the best show of the night by far.

After my performance, I work my way through the crowd to the man with the ponytail and black glasses and I sit on his lap. I smile and I say "Hi my name is Precosia." I look at him and felt his cock harden on my ass. He smiled and gave me a thousand dollars; I proceeded to give him a lap dance. Then someone yanks me from me from behind and says, "What did I tell you, Wendy!"

It was Dan. OMG! What in the fuck is he doing? I said, "What??!!!! He gave me a thousand dollars for a lap dance!"

He said, "I don't give a shit how much he gave you. He pulls my hair and and looked me in my eye. Do you understand what I am saying?" he yells.

The handsome guy was just staring in shock at this drama in shock. He started to say something but Dan said, "Hey, stay out of this. I'm her boss and this is House rules."

I break away and go backstage to get dressed. Dan follows and tries to pacify me, his hands trying to hold my shoulders.

I shopping mad. "Don't touch me. I quit!"

"You can't quit. I will find you." He says as if to threatened me.

I walk out the front door and walk home. Then I realize it was still early and I didn't want to hear mom yelling, so I stop at McDonald's to get something to eat and pass some time away.

When I got home, I hear screams coming from my mom's bedroom. Her boyfriend Tim is beating her with his fists and she lay bloody on the bed.

Hey, stop hitting her!" I screamed. I pick up a vase and hit him on his face; he grabs me and I break lose and run to kitchen and get a knife. I reach to stab him when my mom gets in front of me and yells, "No Wendy."

I accidentally end up stabbing my Mom in her chest. She falls to the floor and he picks her up and cradles her in his arms.

I scream, "Please wake up mommy, don't die! I need you." Tears run down my face and I see mom's take her last breath.

After the police investigation, I was found innocent and my mother's boyfriend was charged with involuntary manslaughter.

The week that followed was terrible, I had to make funeral arrangments. I had no relatives and no one to help me. I was sad and wanted to die. I killed my mother trying to save her. It was all so wrong.

It was a small funeral, there was hardly anyone there. My mother didn't have any friends and we had no relatives.

I see a man standing outside the cemetary. He looked ever so familiar to me. As I made my way out of the burial ground, he came forward and expressed his condolence. "I'm truly sorry for your loss, Wendy, saw it on the news. My name is Jake Turner. "Do you rememeber me from the club, you gave me a lap dance?"

I said, "Oh, yes, I remember you." Oh wow. What on earth was he doing here.

"I'm a cop. I know that you're underage and working at the Gentleman's Club–"

It was like something hit me lightening quick. I was both in awe and in shock. "Excuse me, are you here to arrest me?"

"No, I'm not going to arrest you. I want to help you. You could be in danger. Here's my card, call me as soon as possible."

I called him the next day, and we met for lunch.

He said, "Hi Wendy, thank you for coming.

I want to be honest with you. I'm a private detective, and I'm investigating the Gentleman's Club. I've been hired by a client whose daughter is missing. We believe your boss is involved in organized crime, trafficking young girls aged 14-16 years and selling them overseas."

"Omg, really?" This was some serious stuff.

"I need your help to bring them down." He said.

"So, you want me to rat on Dan?"

"Yes, I want you to help me and do the right thing. These are young girls that are kid-napped and most will never see their parents again unless we bring the criminals to justice."

"Okay, I understand." I say trying to comprehend the gravity of it all.

"Have you heard or seen anything suspicious?"

"I've overheard some girls talking about it, though it wasn't completely clear. I was supposed to be taken away like that but then I quit the same night I'd given you the lap dance.

"Okay, will you help me?" he asked.

"Alright, I will. I don't want to go to jail. What do you want me to do?"

"I want you to keep your ears open and call me whenever you hear something."

The next day, I report to work to the surprise of most. Everyone expressed their sympathies. I finally meet up with Dan. "Welcome back, sorry about your mother. We'll talk later." He said dismissively.

I said, "Okay," and he walked into his office with three other men.

I hadn't worked in a couple of weeks and was anxious to get started. I change to a black short lacy dress, it was sexy and skin tight. It snaps from the back. When the announcer introduced me, the crowd went crazy, all the regulars remembered me. I walked on the stage like I owned the place, swaying my body to the music and running my fingers through my hair. I remove my dress, very slowly and take off my bra. Then I bend down with only my thong on, holding the pole.

I finished the set and head backstage to get dressed. I hear Dan talking in his office.

"I'll give you $10,000."

Dan says, "She's 15, long blond hair and blue eyes. I won't take less than $20K." he says with a laugh.

"Okay, when will you bring her?"

"I already have the passport and visa. I'll book the flight for next week."

I decided to leave before someone sees me. I have another show in 2 hours. So I go back on the floor and mingle with the crowd. Thirty minutes later I see Dan talking to the same guys in the VIP section. So I decide to sneak into his office and see what I can find... and bingo! I see a flight for two people booked for Cabo, Mexico. I couldn't remember the names or flight information, but I did remember Cabo Mexico because we had been there on a family vacation when my father was alive. I finshed my routine and then head home eager to make a call to Jake. It wasn't much information as I couldn't remember the eaxct date. I call Jake and convey all I could remember.

He said, "Thank you, Wendy, I will see what we can do with it and if you hear anything else let me know but please be safe." He said

and ended the conversation.

FEAR OF THE MIND

Three weeks went by and I didn't hear or see anything else suspicious. Then one night just before I was getting dressed to leave to go to the club, I was shocked when I watched the news.

Flight Attendant saves 14-year-old girl from Human Trafficking in route to Cabo Mexico. Sky Blue Airlines vet Moxxy Jonhson noticed a disheveled girl with greasy blonde hair sitting with a well-dressed older man who boarded with her in San Franscico. She looked as if she was homeless and hadn't slept in days. During the flight I kept trying to make eye contact, but she always looked away or kept her head down. I just felt that something wasn't right. And then one time I passed by and she looked me in my eyes. I didn't know for sure, maybe it was just my intuition but I thought something was wrong. I didn't want to make the man suspicous by asking if she was alright, so when I served them a beverage, I gave her a pad and pencil to play a game called "Connect the Dots." I figured if something was wrong she could write a note. Later as we were about to make our descent, I went over to her and said would you like to use the restroom and the man spoke up and said, "Yes she would."' I directed her to the first class restroom so I could keep an eye on her, but the man went and waited for her by the door. I also, waited to make sure no one else would go inside the restroom until I checked to see if she left a note. When she came out of the restroom they returned to their seats. I went inside the restroom and she left a note that said, "Please Help Me!"

I went to the Captain and told him of the situation, and he notified the authorities to meet at tarmac in the airport. When the plane landed, I *made an announcement for the passengers to stay in their seats as we have a situation and it would take a few minutes to resolve. The authorites came on board and apprehended the human trafficker.*

OMG! The man was Dan Cooper from the "Gentleman's Club'! He was caught red handed human trafficking a girl.

Later, I would find out that the arrest had nothing to do with the information I had given, that it was good intuition on the part of the flight attendant because someone gunned down private detective Jack Turner in a drive-by as he sat at a stoplight, just hours after I talked to him.

Shaken by the news, I learned a valuable lesson–that it could have been me, dead or missing. I felt God was trying to tell me something. You can't do wrong and think you are going to get away with it. I quit dancing and changed my life & got on the right path. I went to college and graduated. I'm now 32 years old–and work as a Social Worker helping the poor & the downtrodden find their way. My favorite song is "God's going to cut you down. *"You can run on for a long time, but sooner or later God is going to cut you down, you can be working against your fellow man in the dark all you want. God made the black and made the white and what's done in the Dark shall come to light."* ~Johnny   Cash

Fear Control

When fears control your mind, it exercises its right to hold your body and soul captive too; we have to find a way to be kind to ourselves and forgive us for the things that we couldn't get right the first time around. Our mind will play tricks on us as life exposes our weakest spots through the challenges it presents. You'll think you've gone crazy and that no one will understand you, that's when you must embrace the reality of you being enough for YOU. You don't need anyone else to understand you, because you're unique and so is your purpose. Someday the light will shine upon you as you tread this dark road; the lies of the enemy and the human rationale is an unholy allegiance. Because the truth is, that some things are beyond the comprehension of our mortal minds and not everyone is going to understand it. Keep walking, for life isn't about the end game, it's about what you do along the journey and how you overcome your fears with   faith.

Other Titles by Martha Perez

Short Stories

In the Dark

These Eyes Have Seen

Novels

Broken Pieces

Broken Heart

Broken Dreams

About the Author

Martha was born and raised in Los Angeles, CA. She now lives in West Covina, CA with her husband Sal Andalon and their dog, Sugar Bear. She has a son, a daughter and two granddaughters. Her hobbies include reading, writing, exercise and long walks. 'Broken Pieces' is her first book, which is followed by 'Broken Heart', and a, third book Broken Dreams, an accomplishment she is very proud. She also co-authored a short story book with M LeMont titled These Eyes Have Seen.

www.marthaperez.info
www.brokenpieces.rocks
TWITTER: @MarthaPerezBook

www.ingramcontent.com/pod-product-compliance
Lightning Source LLC
Chambersburg PA
CBHW020549020726
47494CB00006B/1991